Desiree cho[illegible], as she speared the man with her eyes.

Mathis Hazard didn't even have the good grace to appear sheepish or apologetic. "Ex-wife," he corrected. "Well, almost."

Her voice rose half an octave. "Almost?"

"We've been separated."

Desiree continued to stare at him. "Have we?"

Mathis was, apparently, a teller of tall tales. "But the divorce hasn't gone through yet." He grinned at her. "We're still hoping to work it out."

As Desiree looked at him in unrestrained wonder, she heard the voice of Miss Mays, one of her guests.

"We're all rooting for you, Miss Stratford. Or should I say…Mrs. Hazard?"

Dear Reader,

Why not sit back and relax this summer with Silhouette Desire? As always, our six June Desire books feature strong heroes and spirited heroines who come together in a highly passionate, emotionally powerful and provocative read.

Anne McAllister kicks off June with a wonderful new MAN OF THE MONTH title, *The Stardust Cowboy.* Strong, silent Riley Stratton brings hope and love into the life of a single mother.

The fabulous miniseries FORTUNE'S CHILDREN: THE BRIDES concludes with *Undercover Groom* by Merline Lovelace, in which a sexy secret agent rescues an amnesiac runaway bride. And Silhouette Books has more Fortunes to come, starting this August with a new twelve-book continuity series, THE FORTUNES OF TEXAS.

Meanwhile, Alexandra Sellers continues her exotic SONS OF THE DESERT series with *Beloved Sheikh,* in which a to-die-for sheikh rescues an American beauty-in-jeopardy. *One Small Secret* by Meagan McKinney is a reunion romance with a surprise for a former summer flame. Popular Joan Elliott Pickart begins her new miniseries, THE BACHELOR BET, with *Taming Tall, Dark Brandon.* And there's a pretend marriage between an Alpha male hero and blue-blooded heroine in Suzanne Simms's *The Willful Wife.*

So hit the beach this summer with any of these sensuous Silhouette Desire titles…or take all six along!

Enjoy!

Joan Marlow Golan
Senior Editor, Silhouette Desire

THE WILLFUL WIFE

SUZANNE SIMMS

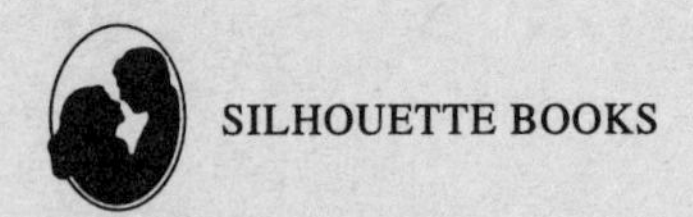

ISBN 0-373-76224-0

THE WILLFUL WIFE

This edition published by arrangement with Harlequin Books S.A.

Look us up on-line at: http://www.romance.net

Printed in U.S.A.

Books by Suzanne Simms

Silhouette Desire

Moment in Time #9
Of Passion Born #17
A Wild, Sweet Magic #43
All Night Long #61
So Sweet a Madness #79
Only this Night #109
Dream Within a Dream #150
Nothing Ventured #258
Moment of Truth #299
Not His *Wedding!* #718
Not Her *Wedding!* #754
**The Brainy Beauty* #850
**The Pirate Princess* #862
**The Maddening Model* #923
**The Willful Wife* #1224

*Hazards, Inc.

SUZANNE SIMMS

had her first romance novel published fourteen years ago and is "thrilled" to be writing again for Silhouette Desire. Suzanne has traveled extensively, including a memorable trip to the Philippines, which, she says, "changed my life." She also writes historical romance as Suzanne Simmons. She currently lives with her husband, her son and her cat, Merlin, in Fort Wayne, Indiana.

One

She was a looker.

Mathis Hazard handed the photograph back to the gentleman on the other side of the desk and told him as much. "She's a good-looking woman."

"Desiree is beautiful and we both know it," George Huxley stated as he leaned back in his executive-style, ergonomically-correct leather chair. He steepled his fingers under his chin and studied the picture that occupied one corner of his desk.

No doubt former Ambassador Huxley saw in the black-and-white studio portrait what Mathis had seen: a young Grace Kelly type, right down to the long, lithe legs, the patrician features, the flawless complexion and the shoulder-length blond hair.

Yup, she was a looker, all right.

Mathis decided to concede the point. ''She is beautiful.''

''To tell you the truth the photograph doesn't do Desiree justice,'' the older man claimed, running his hand back and forth along his chiseled jawline. It was some time before he added, almost as an afterthought, ''She's a Brahmin.''

Mathis managed to keep a straight face. ''As in bull?''

''As in Bostonian.'' George Huxley went on to explain. ''Desiree was born and bred in Boston. She has the right pedigree. She attended all the right schools. She traveled in all the right circles. She traveled *to* all the right destinations—Paris, Florence, Venice, Rome. Naturally she studied all the right subjects.''

''Naturally,'' Mathis echoed. He wondered exactly what constituted the ''right'' subjects for a Boston blue blood.

His companion turned out to be a mind reader. ''Art history, classical music, foreign languages.''

Mathis grunted.

George Huxley continued. ''Desiree lives at the right address, works at the right place, even wears the right designers. Nothing flashy, of course. Mostly Chanel or Armani.'' The distinguished sexagenarian behind the rosewood-inlaid desk paused and drew a breath. Then he shook his head from side to side and admitted, ''Damned, if she doesn't do all the right things.''

''So what's the problem?''

"According to her parents—and it's her parents who contacted me—my goddaughter *did* all the right things."

Mathis couldn't help but notice the use of the past tense. "I repeat, what's the problem?"

"The Hotel Stratford."

His brow crinkled into a studied frown. "The Hotel Stratford here in Chicago?"

"The very one."

Mathis had only been in town a week but he'd heard of the Stratford. "It's a landmark."

"More like an albatross," his client confessed. "The founder was Desiree's great-grandfather, Colonel Jules Stratford, late of His Majesty's Bengal Lancers. Colonel Stratford served King and country in India well over half a century ago. Apparently the gentleman felt if he could command a regiment, he could run a hotel. He retired from the military, emigrated to this country, bought an old hotel, which he refurbished, and named it the Stratford."

"After himself?"

"Yes. Anyway, the Stratford was once *the* premier small hotel in Chicago. Then the Colonel got older and began to fade, as we all do, and the hotel did likewise. The gentleman passed away some twenty years ago. His widow—she was his second wife, his first preceded him in death—tried to keep up with the business, but it became more difficult with each passing year." George Huxley paused for perhaps a quarter of a minute. "Anyway, Charlotte died a few months ago and Desiree inherited the Hotel Stratford, lock, stock and dilapidated barrel.''

Mathis waited. He was good at waiting.

''Desiree is an adult. She can spend her time and money any way she wishes to,'' Ambassador Huxley declared. ''That is her prerogative.''

Mathis agreed.

''However, her parents are concerned that she is allowing sentiment to override her usual practical nature. I've reminded them that their daughter is not only beautiful, but amply endowed with brains.'' In an aside, the man said, ''She graduated magna cum laude from my own alma mater, Harvard.''

Mathis was suitably impressed.

George Huxley picked up the thread of his conversation. ''I have also pointed out to her mother and father that Desiree's whole life has been spent preserving the past.'' The one-time ambassador stroked his chin as if he were tugging on an invisible beard. ''It's no doubt the reason Desiree is so good at what she does.''

''Which is?''

''She's a curator for the Boston Museum of Fine Arts. Her specialty is document preservation.''

Mathis stared at the black-and-white photograph again. Strange, the woman didn't look boring.

''Anyway, my goddaughter has taken a leave of absence from the museum and is now here in Chicago, trying to find a way to restore the Stratford to its former glory. Frankly, none of us believes Desiree realizes what she's let herself in for. That's why I called on Jonathan and Hazards, Inc. for help.'' It was another minute or two before the former diplomat said, ''Your cousin once did me a great favor.''

''Jonathan was the special agent who smuggled you out of Beirut,'' Mathis stated matter-of-factly.

That brought a raised eyebrow from the man behind the desk. ''Yes.'' It was no more than ten seconds before George August Huxley's curiosity obviously got the better of him. ''Although it was a long time ago, I can't imagine Jonathan telling anyone, not even his own family, about the mission.''

''He didn't.''

''Then how did you know?''

Mathis shrugged his shoulders. ''I used to know a lot of things back in the old days.''

His companion thumped his knee and laughed out loud. ''Back in the old days?'' Robust laughter filled the office. ''How old are you? Thirty-five? Thirty-six?''

Mathis gave a semblance of a nod. The renowned emissary to several of the world's trouble spots had hit the nail neatly on the head. Mathis had turned thirty-six on his last birthday.

''You Hazards are all alike.'' Despite his many years of diplomatic experience, and nearly as many as the driving force behind the Kemet Museum in Chicago, George Huxley evidently couldn't make heads or tails of the Hazard clan.

The ambassador wouldn't be the first person who had found his family, with its assortment of brothers, half brothers, cousins and nephews confusing, Mathis acknowledged. Confusing *and* intimidating, if the truth be known.

"I assume that's a compliment," he said.

The white-haired gentleman came forward in his chair and rested his elbows on the edge of the desk. "Of course it is. There isn't a man I admire, or trust, more than Jonathan Hazard. Hell, if push comes to shove, I want Jonathan on my side."

"He was." Mathis absently brushed at the brim of the hat he was holding in his left hand. "He still is. But I'm sure he considers the debt long repaid, especially since the 'situation' involving the Egyptologist and the Egyptian antiquities."

"Marrying Samantha Wainwright was an added benefit of that assignment," the older man offered up with a delighted smile. "I understand that Jonathan is on paternity leave."

Mathis returned the smile. "He's taken several months off to spend with Samantha and their new baby."

"Where's Nick?"

"On his honeymoon with Melina."

"And Simon?"

"Simon was never really part of the agency. Besides, he just got back from Thailand."

"With a wife, I hear."

"He married Sunday Harrington."

George Huxley leaned back again, raised his eyes toward the ceiling and drummed his fingers on the arm of his chair, keeping tempo with his own words.

"Sunday Harrington? Sunday Harrington? The name sounds familiar."

"Sunday was a model. *Sports Illustrated.* Now she's a successful fashion designer."

"So while the others are out of the office, you've been left in charge of Hazards, Inc.?"

"Let's just say I agreed to come to Chicago for a couple of months and keep an eye on things," Mathis said, crossing one leg over the other and plucking a nonexistent speck of lint off his jeans. His jacket was weathered brown leather. His shirt was starched and white. His tie was a southwestern bolo with a gold nugget the size of a thumbnail. His cowboy boots were polished to a mirror sheen.

All dressed up and no place to go.

"I hear you're pretty good."

Mathis shrugged his shoulders and made a noncommittal sound. Since his reputation always seemed to precede him, he rarely found it necessary to mention his credentials.

The former ambassador sought confirmation of his facts. "Army Rangers."

Mathis nodded.

"Border patrol."

He nodded a second time.

"A few covert operations for the government."

Mathis lifted his shoulders and then lowered them again. Appropriately, it was neither a confirmation nor a denial of the gentleman's statement.

"Then private surveillance and security for some of the leading heads of state."

Another movement of his head.

"You get around."

"I get around."

"You're still alive."

"I'm still alive."

"Unscathed?"

There was a moment of hesitation. That was inevitably the question. Had he come out of it unscathed?

Mathis decided to give the socially acceptable answer. It was the only thing he could do. "Unscathed."

Shrewd gunmetal gray eyes assessed him from beneath snowy-white eyebrows. "Good."

It was time to get down to business. "What do you want me to do, Ambassador?" he inquired.

"I want you to check it out," he replied.

"The hotel or your goddaughter?"

George Huxley was blunt. "Both. I hear you're a pretty good businessman as well as an ex—" one hand drew random circles in the air "—whatever-you-are. I want you to find out if Desiree is getting in over her head, if she knows what she's doing."

There was more. Mathis could hear it in the cultured voice. "And...?"

The retired diplomat took in a deep breath and then slowly released it. "And..."

The infinitesimal hairs on the back of Mathis Hazard's neck stood straight up on end. "And what?" he inquired, almost certain he didn't really want to hear the answer.

There was another moment of hesitation, this time on the part of George Huxley. ‘‘There have been several incidents.’’

‘‘Incidents?’’

‘‘Unexplained occurrences.’’

‘‘Such as?’’ Mathis prodded.

The distinguished-looking man appeared almost embarrassed to say. ‘‘Furniture moving.’’

‘‘Furniture moving?’’

‘‘By itself.’’ He continued, albeit reluctantly. ‘‘Strange noises in the night. Glimpses of someone—something—but nothing is ever there.’’

Mathis was amused. ‘‘Are you trying to tell me that the Hotel Stratford is haunted?’’

‘‘I can’t.’’

‘‘Why not?’’

‘‘I don’t believe in ghosts.’’

‘‘That makes two of us, because neither do I.’’

‘‘Then you’re just the man for the job. You’ll be a sane voice in an otherwise insane world.’’

‘‘Is there anything else?’’

Huxley squirmed in his seat. ‘‘Well, now that you mention it, there is one more thing.’’

Somehow Mathis had known there would be.

‘‘My gut instincts tell me that this is an inside job,’’ the older man confided to him. ‘‘No one other than my goddaughter must know who and what you actually are. Otherwise, I’m afraid that we’ll never get to the bottom of it.’’

He waited for George Huxley to get to the point.

‘‘You’ll have to go undercover.’’

Mathis made certain his voice was devoid of any inflection. ''You want me to go in disguise.''

''Something like that.''

He arched a quizzical brow. ''Any suggestions?''

Observant eyes glanced from the expensive black Stetson, with its hammered-silver hatband, resting on Mathis's right knee down to his highly polished, hand-tooled black leather boots. ''You could always go as a cowboy.''

Mathis didn't crack a smile. ''What would a cowboy be doing at the Stratford?''

''We'll think of something.''

''We?''

''I'm certain that between the two of us we can come up with a suitable cover story.''

Mathis was certain they could, too. ''When would you like me to start?''

''Today.''

Mathis gazed out the expanse of office windows toward downtown Chicago. He wanted—no, he needed—some information on the Hotel Stratford and its former *and* current owners before he presented himself to the lady from Boston.

''Tomorrow,'' he finally proposed to his distinguished client. ''There are a few details I want to check out before I drop in on Ms. Desiree Stratford.''

''Tomorrow, then,'' the other man agreed.

Some fifteen minutes later they concluded their conversation and Mathis was personally escorted to the door of the elegant office.

George Huxley shook his hand in parting. "Good luck, Hazard," the ambassador said to him.

The unspoken words hung in the air between the two men: *You'll need it.*

The penthouse he was living in for the summer, courtesy of Hazards, Inc., was on the forty-second floor of a Chicago high-rise. It was glass on three sides and had a panoramic view of Lake Michigan.

The evening light was stealing across the unusually placid surface of the great lake. As far as the eye could see it was dark blue water dotted with white sailboats.

The scene somehow reminded Mathis of the view from his adobe casita at sunset, watching the Sangre de Cristo Mountains turn blood red in one of New Mexico's strangely transcendental landscapes.

That New Mexico was all about light was something he had discovered several years ago. Maybe it was why he had picked the location he did when he had started to buy up land in anticipation of the day he would retire from the business.

Mathis raised a can of ice-cold beer to his mouth and took a drink. There was no sense in getting maudlin about his past. No sense in brooding about it. The past was the past. His past was like anyone else's in that it couldn't be changed. And since no one was promised a future, that left only the present. So he concentrated on living in the here and now.

Besides, as he had reassured George Huxley during their meeting that afternoon, he had emerged from his past unscathed...or pretty damned close to it.

"Close only counts in horseshoes and hand grenades, son," came the words of Argos Hazard, one-time rancher, one-time soldier and lawman, sometime husband and father.

Maybe his father had been right, after all.

There were certainly those who would say Mathis Hazard had always been a loner and that's why he was so good at what he did. Mathis knew his past set him apart, made him different from other men, made him alone, made him a loner.

He hadn't thought it odd to buy a ranch in the middle of New Mexico, located between a range of isolated mountains and a secluded lake, away from civilization, his nearest neighbors a good forty miles in any direction. Lord knows, he'd had enough of so-called civilization to last him a lifetime.

It wasn't that he had been around too many people. It was the people he'd been around and the world he'd lived in, a world most people were unaware even existed.

It was a world where a man acquired eyes in the back of his head if he wanted to survive. It was a world where nothing was what it seemed to be, where no one was *who* they appeared to be. It was a world where a man learned to trust only one person—himself—where experience, gut instincts and sheer bravado sometimes saved a man when intelligence alone never would, never could.

He'd always essentially been alone, Mathis recognized. He always would be. At least in New Mexico there was no pretense about it.

He took another swig of his beer.

Female companionship...well, that, as they said, was another matter altogether.

Mathis rubbed the icy can across one cheek, along his jawline and halfway down his neck. He felt rather than heard someone come up behind him. He spoke without turning around. ''Know anything about women, Beano?''

''They're more trouble than they're worth, boss.''

Beano should know. He'd been around the corral a few times in his day. He had married and divorced three women—maybe it was four—and had had a few flings in between that had never made it as far as the altar. He was currently footloose and fancy-free.

William ''Beano'' Jones had hired on at the old Circle H at the age of nine. He'd spent the next half-dozen years working on a chuck wagon for Mathis's grandfather before being promoted to bunkhouse cook. Eventually he had been moved into the kitchen at the ''big house.'' Somewhere along the way he had started to keep an eye out for the ''boy.'' Now Beano was seventy if he was a day, and he still considered it his personal duty to look after Mathis.

Only the boy, of course, had become a man, a man who had been around the corral a few times himself. He'd never officially been roped, hog-tied and branded, Mathis mused, reflecting on his own marital state...or the lack thereof.

He had imagined himself in love once, a long time ago. He'd been nineteen. She had been eighteen, pretty, blond, wild like the wind. It had been a typical summer romance—hot and fast and furious. And then it had been over just like that.

Mathis gazed out on what he knew was a sweltering Chicago night. "What about a lady from Boston?"

"Worst kind of all, boss."

"Why?"

He could sense Beano shifting his weight from one foot to the other. "A woman like that can make a man feel dis-com-bob-u-lat-ed." The word was broken up into its separate syllables. "A woman like that can make a man feel like he's meetin' himself comin' and goin'. She can make him forget."

Mathis was curious. He turned his head. "Make him forget what?"

Beano flashed his trademark grin, the one that drew his mouth up into a bow and sent sparks flying in his dark chocolate-brown eyes. "I've plumb forgot."

Mathis laughed out loud, spilling cold beer onto his bare chest. "I walked right into that one, didn't I?"

"You always were easy pickin's, boy." It was a minute or two before Beano added another pearl of masculine wisdom. "Women," he muttered under his breath, "can't live with them..."

"Yes...?"

Beano left it at that.

Mathis couldn't have agreed more. Knowing that the older man wouldn't ask, he volunteered where he had been that afternoon. "I interviewed a client today."

"Did you?"

"George Huxley."

Beano made a sound in the back of his throat. Mathis knew he wasn't uninformed, just unimpressed that the security agency's latest client was a well-known American diplomat.

"He wants me to look after his goddaughter."

"She the lady from Boston?"

"Yes."

"Smells like trouble to me."

It smelled like trouble to Mathis, too.

"I have to take the case on behalf of Hazards, Inc.," he said, reaching up with the T-shirt in his hand and wiping it across his chest. "I don't have any choice."

"S'pose not."

Mathis put the can of beer down and tugged the damp T-shirt on over his head. He stood there staring out at the lake—was that mist or steam rising from its surface?—and blew out his breath expressively. "She's a real looker."

"They always are." Beano finally spoke up. "If you need any help..."

It was the opening Mathis had been waiting for. "As a matter of fact, I do."

Apparently his cook-cum-self-appointed guardian

angel was in his official mode. "What do want me to do, boss?"

"Tomorrow morning I'd like you to shave extra close and put on your best bib and tucker."

Beano glanced down at his well-washed shirt and jeans, then lower to his well-worn everyday boots. "S'pose that means my best cowboy boots, too."

"And your best hat."

"The white Stetson?"

"Yup."

"You wearing white, too?"

He nodded.

Beano raised one eyebrow. "Out to impress the lady."

Mathis watched his own reflection in the wall of glass. There was a flash of white teeth against tanned skin. "We want to make sure she recognizes right off that we're the good guys."

Beano grinned from ear to ear. "We could just tell Miss—?"

"Stratford. Desiree Stratford."

"We could just tell Miss Stratford that we're the good guys," he suggested.

Mathis absently rubbed his hand back and forth along his nape. "She might not believe us."

The longtime cook made a face. "I said it once and I'll say it again. It smells like trouble."

He had and it did.

The old man's weathered brow crinkled into a dozen distinct frown lines. "Where we goin'?"

Where were they going? How could he explain the

situation to Beano without saying too much or too little? How could he make the other man understand?

Mathis raised the can to his mouth and finished off his beer. Hell, he wasn't sure he understood himself.

Then the words of an old and familiar American folk song started running through Mathis Hazard's head.

Froggy went a-courtin', he did go.
Froggy went a-courtin', he did go.

"We're going a-courtin'" was his answer.

Two

The siren awakened her from a dead sleep.

Desiree Stratford rolled over onto her side, reluctantly opened her eyes and squinted at the clock on the bedside table.

Three in the morning.

"Ohh," she softly groaned, turning her head and burying her face in the goose-down pillow.

She didn't want to be awake. In fact, she wanted desperately to be asleep.

After a day of seemingly endless meetings with lawyers and bankers, architects and contractors, even a delegation of longtime hotel guests, after a dinner of thoroughly atrocious *and* utterly cold food—Desiree vowed she would fire the temperamental and incompetent chef, Andre, just as soon as she had the time to hire a replacement—after an evening spent poring over papers in her great-grandfather's study—had the dear, sweet man kept every scrap of correspondence he had received in his life?—it had been nearly one o'clock, a mere two hours ago, that she had finally crawled, exhausted, into bed.

Now she found herself awake again.

She had no one to blame but herself, Desiree acknowledged. She was the one who had insisted that she move into the oldest wing of the Stratford, into what used to be her great-grandparents' living quarters, into the very bedroom where she had stayed as a child on her thrice-yearly visits to Chicago.

Apparently as a girl she had slept much more soundly than she did at the age of thirty. Now she heard the shrill, jarring, nerve-grating wail of every siren that passed on the street below between the hotel and the busy city hospital nearby.

There was no sense in crying over spilled milk, as her great-grandfather used to say.

It was too late.

It was done.

It was in the wee, small hours of the night and she was wide-awake.

Desiree turned onto her back and stared up at the ceiling overhead. A faint light was coming from the row of windows on the far side of the bedroom, just enough light so that she could make out the shapes and patterns of the mural painted on the ceiling decades earlier by a starving yet talented artist.

The images had faded somewhat with time and the

inevitable layer of dust and grime that had accumulated, but they were still a magnificent rendering of the heavens, complete with sun and moon, stars and planets, clouds and constellations.

The images might have faded, but not her memories...never her memories.

"I'm afraid of the dark, Great-Grandpapa," she confessed one night as she was being tucked into bed.

"But only when it's dark can we gaze up at the sky and see all the stars," he pointed out to her.

Desiree had never thought of that.

"How many stars are there in the sky?" she asked, excited as only an eight-year-old can be excited.

"Thousands. Millions," her great-grandfather answered from his leather wing chair, the same leather wing chair that had always stood alongside the guest bed.

"Can I count them?"

"Of course you can. You can do anything you put your mind to. Anything at all. Don't ever forget that, Desiree."

She gazed up at the painted mural. "But there are so very many stars, Great-Grandpapa."

"Don't worry, child. We'll count them together."

So she and her great-grandfather had counted aloud, her little girl's half-whisper in unison with his great, booming baritone, until she couldn't keep her eyes open no matter how hard she tried. Night after night she would fall asleep to the sound of his voice and dream about places she had never been and things she had never seen.

The decor of the guest room had been something out of a dream, as well. In fact, it still was. It had remained essentially unchanged over the years.

The furniture was delicately carved and inlaid with rare woods from the Jodhpur region of India. Above the bombe bureau were framed pictures of elephants with their trunks majestically raised skyward, mischievous monkeys at play, colorfully plumed birds perched on tree branches and king cobras, hooded, coiled, sinuous, deadly, yet worshiped by a segment of the Indian population as gods.

A large painting hung over the fireplace. It depicted a fierce Bengal tiger with a royal hunting party in pursuit. On the opposite wall was a seventeenth-century embroidered tapestry, stitched with silk thread and illustrating the life of a maharajah, the beautiful ladies of his court, his grand palace and riches beyond imagination.

The family's living quarters had always been filled with personal mementos, keepsakes and souvenirs of the Raj in India. For Desiree they had been a glimpse into her great-grandfather's world, into a world that was gone and would not come again. Oh, how he had enjoyed telling her stories of his days on the Indian subcontinent and of the times when the sun had never set on the British Empire.

There had been a splendor and grandeur about the Hotel Stratford in those days, although if she hadn't been an impressionable child infatuated with the place perhaps she would have noticed even back then that it was beginning to fade.

But as an eight-year-old she had seen only what she wanted to see. She had loved the hotel's elegantly appointed lobby, its highly polished brass adornments, its marble floors underfoot and its crystal chandeliers high overhead, its sweeping staircase and claret-colored carpeting, its uniformed doorman and imposing majordomo.

Most of all Desiree had loved her great-grandfather, resplendent in a perfectly pressed Savile Row suit, starched white collar and old school tie. In a manner of speaking, the Colonel, as his staff had referred to him, had worn a kind of uniform, too. His closet had been filled with identical suits, collars and ties.

It had been her love for her great-grandfather, and for the Stratford with its rich history and traditions, that had eventually led Desiree to make preserving the past her life's work. She believed that without the past there was no understanding of the present and precious little insight for the future.

She exhaled on a long, drawn-out sigh.

Unfortunately, sentimentality had cost her another good night's sleep. It wasn't the first time. It wouldn't be the last. Not if she went ahead with her plans for renovating the hotel from the ground up.

In truth, the Stratford was a dowdy dowager duchess, a bit threadbare, a bit tattered, a bit—well, perhaps more than a bit—past her prime, but not beyond restoration, not beyond redemption. She could be saved. Desiree was certain of it.

But was she certain in her mind…or only in her heart?

Desiree punched at the pillows behind her head—there were half a dozen of every size and shape, covered with the finest Egyptian cotton pillow slips—and stretched out, arms flung to either side, in the antique iron-frame bed.

She gazed up at the stars twinkling overhead on the ceiling and began to count in a whisper, "One. Two. Three. Four." After some time she wetted her lips with her tongue and continued. "Ninety-seven. Ninety-eight. Ninety-nine. One hundred." She persisted. "One hundred and one. One hundred and two."

Enough was enough.

"There's no sense in pretending any longer," Desiree muttered as she propped herself up against the mound of pillows. "You aren't going back to sleep any time soon."

She was reaching for the lamp on the bedside table when she thought she heard something.

Her hand froze in midair.

She slowly took in her breath and held it. She wasn't sure which came next: the odd, tingling sensation that raised the small hairs on the back of her neck or the soft pad of footsteps outside in the corridor.

There was no one else staying in this wing, no one else with a reason for being here.

Desiree gave herself a good shake. It was the dead of night. The Stratford was an old building. Old buildings went hand in hand with strange noises.

Or maybe it was no more than an overactive imagination on her part. Not that she was a woman prone to an overactive anything, but she was living alone in this section of the hotel.

Truth to tell, there had been more than one unexplained occurrence since her arrival at the Stratford several weeks ago. Furniture had been found mysteriously moved from one room to another. Everyone swore their innocence in the matter, and no one seemed to have any idea of who or why or when or even how this feat could have been accomplished.

Then there had been the glimpses of something—someone—just at the edge of Desiree's peripheral vision, but nothing—and no one—was ever there.

Lastly were the inexplicable noises, always at night, always when she was alone.

Perhaps it was someone up to no good. Perhaps it was someone trying to frighten her. No doubt that's what it was. That's what it had to be.

Shenanigans.

Monkeyshines.

Tasteless practical jokes, in Desiree's opinion.

There were stories, naturally. There were always stories about historic old buildings. She had heard the outlandish ghost stories about the Stratford her very first night back in Chicago. Her resident guests had seen to that.

One account, relayed with particular relish by Miss

Molly Mays, had concerned the ill-fated workman who had fallen asleep during the renovation of the hotel. He had accidentally been buried alive inside a foot-thick brick wall. The poor devil had suffocated to death, of course, before his absence had been noted by his fellow workmen and the wall could be frantically torn down again.

Then there was the tale of the mobster and his moll, related with equal enthusiasm by Miss Maggie Mays. During the era of Prohibition, the couple had apparently been Chicago's version of Bonnie and Clyde. The pair had come to an inglorious, although perhaps deserved, end when they were killed in a barrage of police bullets. Ever since, according to the elder Miss Mays, it had been rumored that the lovers' spirits still roamed the corridors of the Stratford, phantom guns blazing.

Balderdash.

Poppycock.

Pure malarkey, as her great-grandfather would have said. She didn't believe in ghosts. At least not those kind of ghosts, Desiree reminded herself.

Thump.

Thump.

The sound of footsteps came again.

Without switching on the bedside lamp, Desiree threw back the summer-weight covers and sat up. As a girl her feet had dangled over the edge of the high English-style bed. Now they were firmly planted on the cool hardwood floor.

Thump.

"Enough of this nonsense," Desiree grumbled under her breath as she reached for her bathrobe and made a beeline for the door.

Despite the twenty years since her last visit, for she had stopped coming to the Stratford after the death of her great-grandfather, she knew the guest room, and the entire apartment, like the back of her hand.

Without a sound Desiree turned the knob, opened the door a crack and peered out into the corridor. Vintage lights, strategically spaced every ten or fifteen feet, cast a garish glow on the flowered wallpaper and claret-colored carpeting.

She stepped into the hallway and quietly slipped along in her bare feet, double-checking each juncture as she came to it.

There was nothing.

There was no one.

There was no sign of whoever had been there.

Not that Desiree was particularly surprised by the results of her impromptu investigation. She had scarcely expected to peer around the corner and catch the culprit red-handed.

"Utter nonsense," she announced aloud, her voice echoing in the empty corridor. "I'm going to bed."

It was at that moment that Desiree noticed the door to her great-grandfather's study was ajar. Surely she had closed it when she'd finished working for the night.

Hadn't she?

She made a split-second decision. Under the circumstances, she wasn't going to take any chances. Reaching around the corner, Desiree grabbed one of Jules Stratford's traditional English walking sticks from the brass umbrella stand. She firmly grasped the "weapon" in one hand and groped for the light switch with the other.

Flicking the switch, she blinked several times in rapid succession and gave her eyes a second or two to adjust to the change. Then she quickly looked around.

The room was filled with rich mahogany furniture and glass-fronted barrister bookcases, Edwardian-era oil paintings and mementos from her grandparents' days in India, *and* shadows.

Thankfully, the room was also vacant.

Desiree quickly crossed to the opposite side of the spacious study and opened the door into the adjoining parlor. The formal room beyond was also unoccupied.

After closing the parlor door, she turned. At a glance the study appeared to be exactly as she had left it two hours before. She lowered the silver-tipped walking stick and approached the massive mahogany desk. That's when she realized something was amiss.

Desiree spun on her heel and stared at the wall behind the desk where her great-grandfather's sword and dagger, presented to him upon his retirement from active military duty, had been displayed for as long as she could remember.

The dagger was gone.

She was almost certain...she *was* certain...that the dagger had been there earlier that evening.

Who could have taken it?

Why take it?

Where was it now?

Then, out of the corner of her eye, something else caught Desiree's attention. She slowly pivoted. As the object came into focus, a chill spiraled down her spine. For a moment she couldn't think. She couldn't move. She didn't even breathe.

Finally collecting herself, she encircled the desk, all the while being very careful not to touch anything.

Perhaps Uncle George was right.

Perhaps it was a good idea for a security expert to inquire into the peculiar goings-on at the Stratford.

Admittedly, when her godfather had telephoned that afternoon to inform her that he had called in a "hired gun," Desiree had argued the point with him. She had recited to him a dozen good reasons why she didn't want and didn't need extra security at the hotel.

Now she was relieved that she hadn't managed to talk George Huxley out of his plan. As a matter of fact, it was of some consolation to her just knowing that the man was scheduled to show up first thing in the morning.

For there, directly in front of Desiree Stratford, firmly embedded in the top of the desk, its tip neatly slicing through a sheet of thick, cream-colored writing paper embossed with the family coat of arms and with the single word *forewarned* block-printed across its surface, was her great-grandfather's dagger.

Three

Rashid Modi hovered in the doorway of what had once been the night manager's office. He discreetly cleared his throat. ''A thousand pardons, Ms. Stratford.''

Desiree looked up from the most recent financial statement submitted by her accountant—it was *not* good news—and said rather absently, ''Yes, Mr. Modi?''

The hotel manager squared his shoulders. ''There is someone here to see you.''

''Who is it?'' she inquired of the capable young man who had been in charge of the day-to-day operation of the Stratford and its few remaining staff members since the death of her step-great-grandmother, Charlotte, last winter.

"He did not give his name." Rashid Modi remained standing at attention. "He said you would know who he was."

Desiree glanced at the antique cloisonné timepiece on the bookcase opposite the desk. It was precisely eight o'clock. Perhaps her caller was the security expert retained by George Huxley. The security expert she wasn't supposed to mention to anyone, at least not by profession. If so, the man was punctual. First thing in the morning evidently meant first thing in the morning.

Rashid Modi lingered. "You are busy. Do you wish for me to send him away?"

Desiree tidied the stack of papers in front of her and slipped them back into the large official-looking envelope in which they had been delivered the day before. "Thank you, Mr. Modi, but that won't be necessary," she said as she stashed the envelope in her briefcase. "I'll see the gentleman."

"As you wish," he acquiesced.

Desiree sensed a certain hesitation on the part of the Stratford's manager. "What is it, Mr. Modi?"

Rashid Modi was the absolute soul of discretion. He was well-dressed, well-spoken, well trained and well liked. There was no doubt in Desiree's mind that he would go far in his chosen career as a hotelier. In fact, the only surprise to her was that he had accepted a position with the Stratford which was, frankly, no longer on the "A" list of Chicago hotels. The man could have aimed higher, much higher: the Tremont or the Whitehall or even the Raphael, and he could certainly have commanded more money than Charlotte Stratford—and now Desiree—could afford to pay him.

Mr. Modi hemmed and hawed, and then, with a decided flair for understatement, disclosed, "The person waiting to see you isn't exactly a gentleman."

This unexpected announcement got Desiree's attention. "What is he, then?"

The young man paused, brushed at a nonexistent speck of lint on his lapel and said, "A cowboy."

"A cowboy?" Uncle George—as she had called George Huxley for as long as she could remember; he had been one of her father's best friends since their undergraduate days at Harvard—hadn't mentioned anything about a cowboy. Desiree was admittedly curious. "How do you know he's a cowboy?"

Typically a man of few unnecessary words, Mr. Modi gave a succinct answer. "Cowboy boots. Cowboy hats."

Hats?

Desiree frowned. "Is there more than one hat?"

He nodded.

Lack of sleep had finally caught up with her, Desiree realized as she pondered the problem of the hats. Why would a cowboy wear more than one hat? For that matter, *how* could a cowboy wear more than one hat at a time? Surely the man didn't have two heads. A surreal Salvador Dali-like picture formed in her mind.

Aloud, she asked, "Why?"

It was the hotel manager's turn to frown in puzzlement. ''Why what, Ms. Stratford?''

She wasn't making herself understood. ''Why is there more than one cowboy hat?''

''Because there is more than one cowboy,'' he said simply.

Her mouth formed a silent O.

Rashid Modi held up two long, elegant fingers. ''In fact, there are two cowboys.''

''I see.'' Desiree didn't see, but she supposed that was beside the point.

During their telephone conversation yesterday, her godfather had clearly stated that the security expert's name was Mathis Hazard, and that the well-respected security agency he represented was Hazards, Inc. She was quite certain that Uncle George hadn't said anything about a cowboy or a sidekick.

Mr. Modi moved his head back and forth. With the tip of his tongue against the back of his front teeth, he began to make a small clicking noise. It was definitely a sound of disapproval. ''I told the persons in question to go around to the delivery entrance and see Andre.'' The young gentleman paused, raised his nose ever so slightly in the air and sniffed as only an Englishman can sniff. ''But they, well, *he,* insisted on speaking to you personally.''

''He?''

''The formidable one.''

Mathis Hazard must be formidable, indeed. Rashid Modi was not a man easily impressed or intimidated, nor, for that matter, was he prone to exaggeration.

Desiree only hoped and prayed there weren't going to be any unpleasantries between the very English hotel manager—Rashid Modi was of Indian ancestry, but he had been born, raised and educated in London—and a security agent from the American West, judging from the former's description of the latter.

Frankly she had enough on her mind with the coterie of lawyers and accountants, contractors and architects constantly buzzing around her, not to mention the temperamental Andre and the trio of female guests in permanent residence who acted as though they were the ones who actually owned the Stratford.

If that wasn't enough to drive a sane woman to the brink of insanity, there had been the incident of the night before. She had assumed that Mathis Hazard would want to examine the evidence for himself, so she had left her great-grandfather's dagger exactly as she had found it: jeweled handle gleaming in the lamplight, razor-sharp tip embedded in the top of the mahogany desk.

Desiree brushed a hand across her eyes. After discovering the dagger and the note, she had made a thorough search of her great-grandparents' former apartment. Whoever had been there seemed to have vanished into thin air.

Ninety-nine-point-nine percent certain that the culprit didn't have any intentions of returning to the scene of the crime for a second time that night, Desiree had gone back to bed. First, however, she had securely wedged a sturdy chair under the brass doorknob, since there were no locks on the doors in the family wing. Despite this precaution, it had been nearly dawn before she had managed to fall asleep again.

Rashid Modi repeated his initial offer. "I can send the cowboys away, Ms. Stratford, if you don't have time to see them."

"I can spare a minute or two," she said.

"Shall I show them in?" The manager indicated the confines of the small, once elegant and now somewhat threadbare, office.

Desiree politely shook her head and inquired, "Where are the two men?"

Another concise reply was supplied by Mr. Modi. "The lobby."

Desiree pushed her chair back, reached for the tailored jacket to her suit and rose to her feet. "I'll see them in the lobby, then."

The heels of her pumps clicked on the marble floor as Desiree pulled on her jacket and started down the hallway. Once she reached the lobby she paused for a moment, put her head back and gazed up at the ornate ceiling high above her.

The lobby ceiling was done in the grand Victorian style, with intricately carved cornices and molding, and with a second mural by the same artist who had painted the guest room. This time he had chosen to depict mythical creatures of flight from the six-winged angels of the seraphim to round-cheeked cherubs, from exotic birdmen to a snow-white Pegasus.

The pièce de résistance of the front lobby, however, was the chandelier. It was Austrian crystal, weighed more than a ton, dated from the turn of the century when it was originally a gaslight and, since its conversion to electricity, was said to be comprised of more than two thousand individual lightbulbs.

In the hotel's heyday there had been a full-time employee whose job had been to clean and change the bulbs in the lighting fixtures, including the Stratford's prized chandelier. There had also been an attendant who polished, on a daily basis, the brass balustrades on the staircase. And another whose sole duty was to set and wind the clocks, all ninety-seven of them.

That was no longer the case. The ninety-seven clocks were long gone, and the cleaning and polishing were done by a small, independent business firm that had won the job by quoting Charlotte Stratford the lowest bid.

Nevertheless, the myriad stories about the Stratford, its architectural and social history, its famous guests and its somewhat more humble yet interesting employees, had fascinated Desiree when she was a girl. They still did.

Her gaze returned to ground level. There were her early-morning visitors standing in the middle of the lobby. Mr. Rashid was correct, as he usually was. They were cowboys. Both of them.

The next thing Desiree noticed were the white hats. Not on their heads, thankfully, but held at their sides. At least they were gentlemen enough to remove them indoors.

The disparity between the two men was immediately apparent. One was quite short. The other was very tall. The smaller, slightly rotund cowboy was facing her. His features were craggy. His skin was wrinkled and leathery and tanned to the color of toast. Obviously he had spent a lifetime outdoors in the elements. In Desiree's estimation he was the older by a good thirty or forty years, and he was also the more animated of the pair.

The second man was in profile. From this angle Desiree put his age as mid-thirties. He could have been younger or older. She decided he was probably older.

Her eyes swept his appearance from the ground up. He was dressed in cowboy boots, faded blue jeans, a Western-style leather coat and a white dress shirt. He had shunned a traditional tie, as had his sidekick, in favor of a bolo, complete with obligatory gold nugget.

Still, it wasn't the man's conspicuous bolo or his spit-polished cowboy boots or his pristine white cowboy hat that caught and held Desiree's attention. It was something far less tangible. It was something in the way he stood there, motionless, quietly assessing the front entrance, the registration desk, the sweeping staircase, in fact, the entire lobby. It was almost as if he had eyes in the back of his head.

That's when Desiree suddenly realized that he knew she was watching him.

A tingle of awareness tiptoed along her spine. She took in a sustaining breath and discreetly blew it out again. Now she understood why the hotel manager had referred to her visitor as intimidating. The man was more than intimidating. He was dangerous. In fact, he positively reeked of danger. It was tightly held-in-check, controlled danger, but it was danger, nevertheless.

Desiree didn't doubt for a moment that this was a man who could take care of himself wherever he was, that this was a man who knew who his enemies were and who his friends were, and regarded both with equal suspicion. She found herself wondering where in the world Mathis Hazard had been and what he had been called upon to do.

Mr. Hazard was dangerous for another reason, as well, Desiree acknowledged to herself. With those broad shoulders, muscular arms and that chest, with that lean waistline and long legs, he was dangerous to women.

Even *she* wasn't immune, Desiree recognized, although she had never been interested in the "man's man" type before. Her personal preference in the opposite sex was a well-educated, erudite, witty and socially accomplished escort who would accompany her to concerts and plays, gallery showings and charity events.

Yet she couldn't help but notice that Mathis Hazard's hair was luxuriously thick and a rich dark brown in color, that it was a little too long in the back and around his ears, and that it had a tendency to curl at his nape.

Even in profile she could see that his forehead was high and his dark eyebrows were arched. His nose bordered on the patrician, but a telltale bump on the bridge meant it had been broken at some point in his life. His mouth was taut, the lower lip was fuller than the upper. His chin was square and jutted with determination. His ears were slightly small, nicely shaped and tucked close to his head. His hands were large and masculine, yet graceful.

Then he turned his head—just his head, nothing more, nothing less—and she saw his eyes, dark, intelligent, somewhat mysterious, piercing and definitely predatory.

Desiree Stratford had met many men in her life, from temperamental artists to affluent collectors, from the homeless on the streets of Boston to wealthy philanthropists, from heads of state to leaders of industry, even those who claimed royal blood or who were, indeed, royalty. She had known men with that implacable air of self-confidence, men who wore the mantle of power as though they were born with it, men with a core of inner strength that seemed to defy logic.

This was one of those men.

She was suddenly tempted to turn tail and run just as fast and just as far as she could.

''Don't let your imagination run away with itself, Desiree Marie Stratford,'' she chided herself under her breath.

She was no lily-livered female, no fainthearted damsel in distress. She was a modern woman with her own career, her own money, her own apartment and her own life.

She even had her own hotel.

Although Desiree had always had perfect posture, no doubt thanks to the admonitions of her mother as she was growing up—*"No slouching, my dear. Stand tall. Shoulders back. Abdomen in. Chin up. Be proud to be tall, Desiree."*—she breathed in and out, made herself stand even a little taller and squared her shoulders.

Now, what was it Uncle George had told her about the security agent?

He was working undercover. That was it. Mathis Hazard was posing as some kind of relative. Apparently one from the West Coast branch of the family from the way he was dressed.

Under the circumstances, she couldn't march up to him, stick out her hand and say, "Hello, I'm Desiree Stratford. Are you Mathis Hazard?" After all, she was supposed to know this man.

Desiree had hoped that her first meeting with Mr. Hazard would take place in private. There was no chance of that now, for graciously greeting the cowboys, as if they were honored guests, were the Stratford's three remaining permanent residents: Miss Molly Mays and her twin, Miss Maggie Mays, and a former exotic dancer, Miss Cherry Pye. Miss Pye preferred the term *exotic dancer* to *stripper.*

Cherry Pye, nee Cherline Pyle, admittedly now a

bit long in the tooth but still in possession of an enviable figure for a woman who must be sixty or sixty-five years of age, would be the first to tell you she was born and raised in Cicero, one of Chicago's tougher neighborhoods. She wasn't ashamed of her background, she was always quick to say. In fact, she was proud of it.

It seemed that Cherline Pyle had wanted to be a ballet dancer, but there hadn't been any money to pay for dancing lessons. By the age of sixteen she had grown too tall for the ballet, anyway. Not long after, she had legally changed her name to Cherry Pye, gone to work at a local strip joint and the rest was history.

"Good morning, ladies," Desiree called out cheerfully, greeting the three aging women as a group.

This was no small feat when the two Miss Mays were genteel poverty and Miss Cherry Pye was from the wrong side of the tracks. And, in their minds, never the twain shall meet.

"Good morning, Miss Stratford," the three ladies sang out in unison.

The older man stepped forward, white hat grasped in his hands, gave a quick nod and said politely, "It's right nice seeing you again, Miss Desiree."

"Why, thank you," she responded warmly.

"Beano sure has been looking forward to this reunion," chimed in the tall, dark and handsome man.

Desiree placed a careful smile on her face and turned to him. "Mathis, how nice to see you."

The ladies present twittered and chirped like a row of red-breasted robins sitting on a tree branch.

Mathis Hazard looked down at her and smiled. It was a slow, lazy, light-up-the-eyes kind of smile. It was perfect white teeth and an incredibly sexy mouth smile.

Damn, if the man wasn't even more handsome up close than he had been from a distance, Desiree realized. Surely it was a sin for a man to be that handsome.

"Darlin'," Mathis Hazard drawled in a pseudo-Western accent as he covered her hands with his and gently yet insistently drew her toward him.

Darlin'?

She should have suspected trouble right then and there, Desiree registered a moment too late. She should have known the man was up to no good.

Without warning, Mathis Hazard raised his hand, tilted her chin up a fraction of an inch and dropped a kiss on her mouth. It was a quick kiss, no more than a buss really, but she learned a surprising amount in a relatively short period of time.

His lips were warm and his skin was smooth.

His aftershave was subtle, expensive and smelled faintly of wood smoke.

His hands were large, strong and long-fingered, yet they grasped her hands gently.

He was tall. Even taller than she had first thought. The top of her head scarcely reached his chin.

And he tasted...wonderful.

"My, my, that's hardly the way for a man to greet

the woman of his dreams,'' piped up Miss Cherry Pye, who apparently knew about such matters.

''The woman of your dreams?'' Desiree repeated, looking from their incredibly attentive audience, which watched every move they made, to the man standing directly in front of her. ''What have you been telling my guests, Mathis Hazard?''

He gave her an aw-shucks look. ''Why, nothin' short of the truth, sweetheart.''

Sweetheart?

Desiree guarded her expression, but she knew her eyes were glittering.

He went on. ''Now, darlin', there's no sense in keeping our relationship a secret from these nice ladies.''

Sure there was.

''It's all right, my dear. Mr. Hazard has told us who's who and what's what,'' volunteered one of the Miss Mays.

Desiree wasn't sure which Miss Mays had spoken to her. She could never tell the twins apart. They were both white-haired, pink-faced, slightly chubby, past eighty but no one knew just how much past, and they dressed alike. It was easy to confuse the two.

The man beside her opened his mouth. ''*Mathis,* please call me Mathis, Miss Molly.''

Desiree's own mouth dropped open. ''How in the world…?''

''Yes, Mathis has already told us,'' the other Miss Mays, apparently Miss Maggie Mays, informed her.

"Mathis has told you what?" Desiree inquired, trying not to convey her irritation.

"Why he's told us about the two of you, of course."

"That we're related," she said weakly.

They all twittered again.

"You could say so." It was Cherry Pye this time. "At least a man and his wife are related in my book."

Desiree choked on her own saliva. She turned and speared the man with her eyes. "Wife?"

Mathis Hazard didn't even have the good grace to appear sheepish or apologetic.

"Ex-wife," he corrected. "Well, almost."

Her voice rose half an octave. "Almost?"

"We've been separated."

Her hands found her hips. "Have we?"

He was a teller of tall tales. "But the divorce hasn't gone through yet."

"It hasn't?"

He had the unmitigated gall to grin at her. "We're still hoping to patch it up."

"Are we?" Desiree was sorely tempted to say there wasn't a snowball's chance in hell of that.

"We're all rooting for you, Miss Stratford," Miss Molly Mays said, patting her arm reassuringly. Then the elderly woman caught herself. "Or should I say Mrs. Hazard?"

Four

She was the kind of woman who drove him crazy.

True, Desiree Stratford was everything George Huxley had said that she was. She *was* beautiful. She *was* dressed in a tailored suit that he was willing to bet hadn't come off the rack. She *did* exude class and breeding, culture and a privileged education from the top of her sun-kissed blond hair, swept up into a sophisticated chignon, right down to the tip of her toes.

The photograph *didn't* do her justice. Her complexion, like rare porcelain, was opalescent and smooth as satin. Her legs were long and shapely and the nicest pair he had seen in a long time. Her figure was a knockout. She wasn't too thin. She wasn't too round. She had curves in all the right places.

Mathis blew out his breath. Desiree Stratford was a looker, all right. Although in this day and age he supposed it was politically incorrect to notice a woman's physical attributes.

Damned waste, that's what it was.

He went back to his appreciation of her assets. Then there were her eyes. The photograph hadn't done her justice there, either, since it had been in black and white and her eyes were green. Not just an ordinary shade of green but jade-green. Not just jade-green but an exotic luminescent green with hints of amber. He had never seen eyes quite that color before.

Yes, Mathis reflected, Desiree Stratford was everything the ambassador had claimed and more.

And she was the kind of woman who drove him nuts.

He just knew in his gut that she was one of those women who never allowed her hair to get mussed up. He was willing to bet that she was never wrinkled, that she was never frazzled or raised her voice or lost her temper.

He'd give odds that Ms. Stratford was always in control, that she always said and did the right thing. She was the kind of woman who would know which fork to use, even if there were fifty different forks at a table setting. She would know the correct way to do everything from eating ortolan to serving port and Stilton to seating an archbishop to the right of the hostess at a dinner party.

She was cool.

She was cold.

She was self-contained.

She never put a foot wrong. She never put her foot in her mouth. She was perfect.

But she wasn't human.

Mathis was tempted to kiss her again. Not just for show but to prove to her that she was human, that she was no different from the rest of them, that there was a core of passion inside her, even if it was buried deeper than most people's.

He was tempted, but he wouldn't give in to the temptation. This was strictly business and she was a client of Hazards, Inc. via her parents and George Huxley.

She might be the client, but he was the boss.

Nevertheless, Mathis could see that he'd pushed his luck about as far as he dared. Unless he wanted his cover blown sky-high right here and now, he had to get Ms. Stratford away from the trio of ladies watching their every move.

"Ladies," he began politely, addressing their captivated and charmed audience, "I'm sure you understand that Desiree and I have a lot of catching up to do."

It was Miss Cherry Pye, resplendent in bright purple polka dots, with a matching bandanna artfully tied around her henna-dyed hair, who laughed and said, "Is that what it's called these days?"

Mathis gave the small gathering one of his ear-to-ear grins. "Would you please excuse us?"

"Of course," the Miss Mays responded, their myopic eyes twinkling with curiosity.

"Darlin'," Mathis said, taking Desiree Stratford by the elbow and steering her toward the elevators, "we need to go someplace where we can be alone."

"We certainly do," she stated primly.

Ms. Stratford didn't appear the least bit amused by the situation, he noticed. Maybe she was one of those women who lacked a sense of humor or any appreciation for the ridiculous.

Miss Maggie Mays whispered to her twin, her quavering voice clearly carrying across the expanse of the front lobby, "Where are they going, sister?"

Miss Molly Mays responded in the same exaggerated stage whisper, "I don't know, dear."

Wire-rimmed spectacles were nudged up a curious nose by a hand that shook ever so slightly with age. "What are they going to do?"

"Talk, I suppose."

As Mathis turned in the direction of the elevators, he heard a throaty chuckle from Miss Pye.

"They'll communicate," she said, "but I don't suppose there will be a whole lot of talking going on."

"What do you mean?" one of the twins inquired, positively brimming with inquisitiveness.

The woman laughed knowledgeably. "I don't think you're old enough to be told, Miss Mays."

The two Miss Mays stammered with pleasure. "Why, why, thank you, Miss Pye."

Mathis glanced back over his shoulder just as the attention shifted to his old friend, Beano.

"What do you do, Mr. Jones?" inquired Miss Cherry Pye.

"I'm a cook," he told her.

"A cook! How wonderful." She took a step closer to him. "Are you a good cook?"

"My chili recipe won the 'Hot-Damn Best of the Damn-Hot West' contest three years running," he said with all due modesty. Then, in an aside, Beano quickly apologized to both the Miss Mays for the use of his profanity. "If you'll pardon my French."

"It's quite all right, Mr. Jones, we don't speak a word of French," one of the twins reassured him.

Miss Pye brightened. In fact, Mathis was almost certain he saw her licking her lips. "I must confess, Mr. Jones, that the chef here at the Stratford is a disgrace to your profession. We should fire Andre but we can't afford anyone better at the moment." The redhead slipped her arm through his. Somehow her purple dress managed not to clash with her bright red hair. "Tell me, what is your specialty?"

Beano Jones smiled at the woman and answered, "Why, cherry pie, of course."

She giggled.

As Mathis headed for the elevators, the last he saw of William "Beano" Jones, he was being fawned over by the Stratford's three resident spinsters and seemed to be enjoying every moment of it.

Which was good, because Mathis had his hands full, quite literally and figuratively, with Desiree

Stratford. He punched the button for the elevator and the doors slowly yawned open.

They stepped inside. He arched a brow in her direction and the woman sniffed and offered, "Fourth floor."

Mathis pressed the appropriate button and watched as the doors closed in slow motion. Then he immediately released her arm.

Desiree seemed to be biting her tongue and biding her time. Her cheeks were ever so faintly flushed. Her back was ramrod straight. Her expression was rigid. Her body language came through loud and clear: she was still in control, but she was mad as hell.

Frankly, he had expected no less from the moment George Huxley had proposed the guise of ex-husband as the best way for Mathis to get close to his goddaughter and stay close.

He'd warned the ambassador that Desiree wouldn't cotton to the idea. The gentleman had replied that anger was a good thing. Anger would keep Desiree busy. Mathis could deal with her anger just as long as he kept her safe.

Desiree finally opened her mouth. "Was that really necessary?"

"Yes."

"Why?"

He'd keep it simple. He'd keep it truthful. "George and I figured it was a surefire way for us to be together without a lot of questions being asked."

The lady from Boston sniffed. ''I didn't mean that ridiculous story about us being married.''

Mathis frowned in puzzlement. ''What did you mean?''

''The kiss.''

''Oh, that.''

Desiree Stratford turned her head and managed to look down her refined nose at him even though he was considerably taller than she was. ''Yes, that.''

Mathis hadn't intended to kiss her. It hadn't been part of his plan. He wasn't sure what made him do it. He'd acted on impulse. Something he rarely did. Acting on impulse could get a man killed, or at the very least get his face slapped if he wasn't careful.

''Spur-of-the-moment decision,'' he said to her.

Ms. Stratford glanced down at his cowboy boots. ''I'll just bet it was.''

''The ladies seemed to enjoy it.''

''They were the only ones who did.''

''Ouch.'' Mathis unbuttoned his jacket and drove one hand into the pocket of his blue jeans. He jingled his change. ''Look, Ms. Stratford, I've been hired to do a job. It's a job I'm very good at. I'll admit that this case is different from my usual assignment, so I'm making some of it up as I go along.''

She arched her brow. ''Some of it?''

Okay, maybe more than some of it. Maybe he was flying by the seat of his pants with this one, to use an old cliché.

''I'm here to help you and I'm here to see that you remain safe,'' he stated.

"I didn't ask for your help," Desiree Stratford said, tilting her head to one side.

"I know you didn't," he concurred, "but your parents and George Huxley did."

Her voice dripped icicles. "I can take care of myself."

Mathis just bet she could. She could freeze out anybody. "Maybe you can. Maybe you can't," he allowed. "That's for you to know and me to find out." He rubbed his hand back and forth along the nape of his neck, ruffling his too-long hair. He should have taken the time to get a haircut before hitting the Windy City, he realized. "I'm not convinced that there's any real danger involved here, anyway."

Her hand found her hip again. "Really? What makes you say that, Mr. Hazard?"

He ticked off the list on his fingertips. "No threats. No violence. No bodily harm. No blood. No dead bodies, Ms. Stratford."

"That isn't exactly correct," the woman informed him.

"You have dead bodies?"

"No. But there has been a threat." She paused and seemed to reconsider. "Well, an implied threat."

This was news to Mathis. "When?"

"Last night."

"Where?"

"In the family living quarters."

It was time to get down to brass tacks. "Is that where you're staying?"

"Yes."

"Alone?"

She nodded.

Mathis quickly scanned her from top to bottom. It was business—no more, no less. "Were you hurt?"

She shook her head. "No."

"What form did the threat take?"

"I'll let you see that for yourself, Mr. Hazard. I haven't touched anything. It's exactly as I found it in the middle of the night."

Sometimes, in this profession, personal questions had to be asked. "Do you mind telling me why you were awake in the middle of the night?"

"I was awakened by an ambulance siren. Then I thought I heard something."

"Something?"

"Someone." Desiree clarified her original answer by quickly adding "Footsteps."

"Where?"

"In the hallway outside my bedroom door."

"Was your bedroom door locked?"

"No."

That brought his head around. "Why not?"

"There aren't any locks on the doors in the family living quarters." Desiree Stratford seemed to anticipate his next question and went on to explain. "My great-grandparents grew up in an age and in households where servants came and went. They didn't need and they didn't believe in locked doors. They saw no reason for them. The people around them were treated and trusted like family."

"Anyone with a hairpin and a rudimentary knowledge can pick most locks, anyway," Mathis said.

"How reassuring."

"I didn't say it to frighten you, Ms. Stratford. But there's no sense in me giving you a false sense of security, either." Mathis might as well get something straight right here and now. "I will attempt to be as forthright and honest with you as I can be as long as I'm on your case."

"I would appreciate that," she said.

The elevator came to a creaking halt and the doors inched open. There was almost room for three people in the vintage contraption, but not quite. Mathis stepped to one side and let Desiree Stratford exit ahead of him.

He needed to get his bearings. "We're on the fourth floor facing the street. Is that correct?"

"Yes. The best rooms at the Stratford face a small, quiet, central courtyard," she volunteered. "And those rooms are always reserved for guests."

"So, this wing is the family living quarters." It was a statement, not a question.

His client nodded her head again.

"I'd like to see each room as we come to it."

"Of course." Desiree Stratford proceeded to open each door as they progressed down the hallway. "This is, or I should say, this was my great-grandparents' suite—bedroom, sitting room, dressing room and bath." The next door was already ajar. "This is the small kitchen where they made themselves tea or coffee. They took all of their meals downstairs or on trays brought up from the kitchen.''

Mathis made mental notes.

''The guest room where I'm staying.'' It was on the left-hand side of the hallway. ''Next to my bedroom is another guest room, with a bath in between. This is the formal parlor.'' It was on their right. ''And this was my great-grandfather's study.'' The door was open. His guide swept into the room in front of him.

''Very nice,'' Mathis commented as he followed her into the spacious study.

Desiree Stratford ran her hand along the back of an overstuffed chesterfield. ''This was my great-grandfather's favorite room,'' she said, her voice softening.

''I can see why.'' Mathis slowly turned in a circle. ''It's very English.''

''My great-grandparents were originally from India via Herefordshire,'' she told him.

Mathis had figured as much. The knickknacks and paintings were a dead giveaway.

It was time to get down to business. ''Where were you last night when you heard the footsteps?''

''I was in bed.''

''What did you do?''

''I got up.''

''And...?''

''And I came out into the hallway and checked to see if anyone was there.''

''No one was.''

She confirmed his guess. "No one was."

"Then what?"

"Then I saw that the door to the study was open. I distinctly remembered closing it when I was finished working for the night." Desiree Stratford moistened her lips with the tip of her tongue. It was the first sign of nerves he'd seen in the woman. "I decided to investigate. I grabbed one of my great-grandfather's walking sticks, reached around the corner and flicked on the light switch."

"Ill-advised."

"Perhaps."

"'It is better to be prepared and have a strategic plan than to simply react to a situation,'" Mathis stated.

Jade-green eyes were raised and looked at him. "Who, pray tell, said that?"

"General Sun Tzu, although not in those exact words."

"I've never heard of General Sun Tzu."

"He wrote a treatise called 'The Art of War' in about 500 B.C.," Mathis answered.

She crossed her arms. "Is this war, Mr. Hazard?"

"It's a kind of war, Ms. Stratford."

She gave him a speculative glance. "Are you some sort of samurai cowboy?"

Mathis flexed his shoulders. "Samurai were the Japanese warrior class. General Sun Tzu was Chinese." He brought her attention back to the events of the night before. "So you grabbed a walking stick, turned on the lights of the study and..."

''It was empty.''

He wasn't surprised. ''What gave you the impression that someone had left an implied threat?''

''That,'' she said, pointing.

Mathis turned on his heel and walked across the study toward the row of windows. That's when he spotted the exotic dagger stuck in the top of the desk.

''Sonofabitch,'' he muttered under his breath.

Five

"I don't like it," Mathis Hazard admitted as he made a slow, deliberate circle around the mahogany desk, never letting his attention stray from the dagger.

"Neither do I," Desiree said.

Of course, she knew very few people who would like it, who wouldn't be disturbed, or at the very least unhappy, if they discovered a potentially deadly weapon under similar circumstances.

The security expert raised his head and cast a meaningful glance at her. "You didn't touch anything."

Desiree stared straight back into his questioning eyes. "I didn't touch a thing."

He surveyed the situation and gave a preliminary

report. "The dagger was obviously taken from the wall display. The stationery appears to be standard hotel issue."

She confirmed his observations. "The dagger belonged to my great-grandfather, the late Colonel Jules Stratford. It has hung on the wall beside his sword for as long as I can remember. As for the stationery, there is a portfolio placed in each guest room containing writing paper, envelopes and a pen."

Mathis Hazard leaned over and scrutinized the single word printed on the piece of vellum. "'Forewarned,'" he read, straightening. "I assume as in 'forewarned is forearmed.'"

"Actually the quote is simply 'forewarned forearmed,'" Desiree informed him.

He rocked back on the heels of his cowboy boots, cocked a brow and returned her gaze unflinchingly. "Is it?"

She nodded. "It's from Cervantes' *Don Quixote.*"

The man lowered his eyelids and after a moment recited, "'Marriage is a noose.'"

Desiree studied his profile. If that was Mr. Mathis Hazard's true opinion of matrimony, it was little wonder that he was still single. "One of your Western philosophers?"

He raised his redoubtable chin. "It's from *Don Quixote de la Mancha,*" he stated, giving the full title of Cervantes' masterpiece.

His statement surprised her, but she could go one

better than that. "'To give the devil his due,'" she shot back.

Mathis Hazard tossed her an offhanded smile. "Don't tell me. Let me guess. *Don Quixote* again."

Desiree only hesitated briefly before adding, "'Can we ever have too much of a good thing?'"

The man in the Western attire raised his hands in the air in mock surrender. "All right. I give up. You win."

She usually did.

He returned to the business they had been discussing. "Do you have any idea who wrote the note?"

She was adamant. "I have no idea, Mr. Hazard."

"Mathis," he prompted. "I think it's time we dropped the Mr. Hazard and the Ms. Stratford. It's too easy to slip up around other people, and, after all, we're supposed to be married."

Desiree wondered if he really believed they could pull off the charade of a married couple separated but not yet divorced. Then she recalled the brief encounter in the lobby with the two Miss Mays and Miss Pye. In less than a handful of minutes, Mathis Hazard had had no trouble convincing the three women of his cock-and-bull story.

She took in a calming breath. There was no going back now, she acknowledged begrudgingly. If she had intended to call his bluff—and what purpose would that have served her?—she should have done so immediately.

Desiree passed her tongue over her lips. "I agree

that it wouldn't do to slip up and address each other formally in front of the staff or one of the guests."

"It would blow my cover sky-high," Mathis maintained. "It would mean I'd have a lot to explain that I would rather not explain right now." His mouth all but disappeared. "And it would probably guarantee that I'd never get to the bottom of this case."

That cinched it for Desiree.

He returned to the subject of the note. "Is this the first you've received?"

"Yes."

"What do you think it means?"

"I don't know." Desiree explored the possibilities out loud. "Maybe it doesn't mean anything. Maybe it's no more than an idle threat."

The man's attitude was as uncompromising as his words. "All threats should be taken seriously."

Her hand went to her throat. "What if it isn't a threat? What if it was meant to be a warning?"

It seemed that he had decided to play devil's advocate. "Why the dagger, then?"

"As opposed to what?" she asked with a small sigh. "A message scribbled in lipstick on my vanity mirror? An envelope shoved under my bedroom door?"

Apparently Mathis was determined to be the voice of reason. "There are any number of ways to get a message across. Why use such a dramatic, even melodramatic, gesture. A cryptic one-word note of warning with a dagger stuck through it?"

That's when it dawned on Desiree. "To get my attention."

Mathis raised his index finger—the one no doubt referred to out West as his "trigger" finger—and pointed it directly at her. "Bingo," he exclaimed.

"Someone is trying to get my attention."

"That's about the size of it."

"Well, they've succeeded, whoever they were," she said, none too pleased with the message or the messenger.

"Yes, they have."

Her expression and tone of voice were suddenly hopeful. "Then you don't think it's anything to worry about."

"I didn't say that," he countered.

No, he hadn't.

"As a matter of fact," Mathis went on, "as I said, we will proceed in this instance as if there is no such thing as an idle threat. Frankly it has been my experience that what appears to be a trivial matter can sometimes turn out to be a deadly serious one."

She translated it into rudimentary terms. "In other words, better safe than sorry."

"Something like that." Mathis stared at the dagger and the note, then frowned. "It's risky to assume anything in the security business. Besides, I've never cared for loose ends and I've never liked loose cannons." He reached out, grabbed the dagger by its jeweled handle and yanked it from the desk.

Desiree dug her teeth into her bottom lip. "Shouldn't that be dusted for fingerprints?"

A small, mocking smile appeared on his lips. "There won't be any fingerprints."

"Except yours," she quickly pointed out.

"Except mine." Mathis replaced the dagger on the wall behind the desk. "Only an amateur would leave his fingerprints behind and more often than not even a rank amateur wouldn't make that mistake."

Desiree was genuinely curious. "Do you encounter many rank amateurs in your profession?"

"Not in the past." She noticed that he didn't elucidate on exactly what that past had been. "However, these days Hazards, Inc. specializes in executive protection, so we frequently run into disgruntled employees hell-bent on revenge."

Despite the certain forecast of another sweltering summer day in Chicago, Desiree shivered and wrapped her arms around herself.

Mathis gave her a telling look. "That's why we're going to do this by the book."

She wasn't sure what he meant. "Do *what* by the book?"

Mathis ignored her question. Instead he began to pace back and forth, speaking as much to himself as to her. "Sun Tzu spoke of the sheathed sword."

Desiree bit her tongue and kept her eyes at the level of his chest, vowing she wouldn't look even a fraction of an inch lower.

"General Sun Tzu never had to pull his sword because he was a strategist. He wrote in 'The Art of War,' 'True excellence is to plan secretly, to move surreptitiously, to foil the enemy's intentions and balk his schemes so that at last the day may be won without shedding a drop of blood.'" Mathis stopped in front of her. "Do you know what the three keys to effective security are?"

She shook her head.

One finger was held up. "Identify the threat." A second finger was raised alongside the first. "Understand the threat." Then a third finger joined the others. "Plan ahead to avert the threat."

Did that make it as simple as one, two, three? she wondered.

"Protection isn't about guns and it isn't about the use of physical force, Desiree. It's utilizing the brain. It's about thinking." Mathis ran a hand through his dark hair. "That's what we're going to do."

She resisted the urge to snap to attention and salute.

"I've never had a client attacked or harmed," he informed her. "I don't intend to start now."

On some level—considering the source, no doubt a fairly primitive level—the man fascinated her. "I imagine that you're very good at your job."

Mathis hooked his thumbs through his belt loops and spread his feet, solidly planting them a good two or three feet apart. "You'll never know how good," he said without any pretense of modesty.

The man was so self-contained, so self-confident, so sure of himself. He was different from any man Desiree had ever known. In truth, he made her nervous.

After clearing his throat, Mathis said, "We need to get a few things straight."

Her heart began to beat a little faster. "All right."

He didn't move a muscle. "Until this case is solved or the threat is neutralized, I'm the boss around here."

She instantly bristled and opened her mouth to protest. "Now, see here, Mr. Hazard, this is my hotel."

Without blinking an eyelash, he turned on his heel and started toward the door.

"Where are you going?" she called after him.

Mathis Hazard didn't even bother to glance back at her over his shoulder. "I'm leaving," he announced, wrapping a fist around the brass doorknob.

Desiree stared after him in disbelief. "Leaving?"

He paused and stood there broad-shouldered, lean-hipped, long-legged and completely unbending. "Do you want me to leave?" he finally asked.

Desiree breathed in and out. "No."

He turned on a dime and, with eyes the color of a midnight sky, gave her a stony stare. "Do you want my help?"

Desiree realized that she had been issued an ultimatum: *Do it Mathis Hazard's way or do it without him.* What choice did she have? She was in trouble. She needed his assistance. She needed his expertise. She needed him.

She heard herself say the words aloud. "Yes, I want your help."

He still didn't give an inch. "I'm the boss on this

case and you will do exactly what I tell you to do. No complaints. No protests. No questions asked. Is that understood?''

He drove a hard bargain.

Desiree swallowed her pride and nodded her head. ''Understood.''

Mathis returned to the center of the study. ''Good. Let's get started. Who is currently staying in the hotel?''

Desiree gave him the short list of occupants. ''Rashid Modi, the manager. Andre, the chef. Several kitchen helpers. Miss Molly and Miss Maggie Mays. Miss Cherry Pye.''

''Who else?''

''No one else.''

''Do you have a cleaning service?''

''A team of workers comes in once a week to dust and vacuum, scrub and polish,'' she said.

''Only once a week?''

''At the present time we aren't taking any additional guests and the residents understand that's all the Stratford can afford.''

''Are you experiencing financial difficulties?''

Desiree was loath to discuss her business affairs with the man, but she supposed he would have to know the truth before it was all said and done. ''I may have to close down the Stratford or, at the very least, sell it.''

''How do your residents feel about the prospect of losing their home?'' he asked.

''They don't know yet.''

Mathis looked dubious. ''Are you certain?''

Desiree reconsidered. ''They may suspect there's trouble, but they haven't been told anything officially.'' She felt compelled to add, ''Whatever happens, and even I don't know what the final outcome will be, rest assured I won't allow three elderly women to be left out in the cold to fend for themselves.''

''I never thought for a moment that you would,'' he said to her. ''Have you recently fired any staff?''

''No.''

''Any disgruntled ex-employees?''

''Not that I'm aware of.''

''Would you check the records for the past twelve months just to be sure?''

She went a step further. ''I'll also speak with Mr. Modi. He's been the hotel manager since before Charlotte died.''

The tall, dark and handsome man regarded her closely. ''Is there anyone holding a grudge against you personally?''

She thought for a minute, then told him no.

''Think hard, Desiree. I want you to tell me anything that comes to mind, however far-fetched it may seem to you.''

''There is no one with a personal grudge against me, Mathis.''

''I'm looking for a motive.''

She wasn't dense. She'd realized what the questions were about. ''I know you are.''

The man was unrelenting. "You may be the only one with the answer."

She threw up her hands in exasperation. "I don't think I have the answer."

He still didn't stop. "You may have the answer and not even know it."

That seemed highly unlikely to Desiree.

"Let's brainstorm for a few minutes," Mathis proposed, taking a slightly different tack with her. "If the answer doesn't lie in the present, maybe there's a chance that it rests with the Stratford's past."

It wasn't an alien concept to her, the past intruding into the present. She was constantly studying historical "clues" in document preservation. "Go on."

"Your great-grandfather owned and managed the Stratford for more than three decades."

"That is correct."

"I understand that he died nearly twenty years ago."

She nodded.

"Then his widow, Charlotte, ran the Stratford until her own death last winter."

Desiree nodded her head again.

"You are indisputably the heir."

"Indisputably. But no one else would want to bother with the place, anyway," she said crisply. "If you take a good look around you'll notice the 'dry rot and the rising damp.'"

"The Stratford is in need of repairs." His comment was a statement, not a question.

Desiree couldn't prevent the sigh that slipped past

her lips. "The Stratford is in need of extensive and very expensive repairs and a complete renovation."

It was a good thirty seconds before Mathis inquired, "Could the answer lie in your great-grandfather's past?"

"I suppose so."

"Tell me about the Colonel."

Where to begin when Jules Christian Stratford had lived such a long and glorious life?

"My great-grandfather was an extraordinary man who grew up in an extraordinary time and under extraordinary circumstances. He was born on his family's country estate in Herefordshire before the turn of the century. They were landed gentry who lost their land and their wealth before he was twenty. With the last few pennies remaining to his name, he purchased a commission, joined His Majesty's service and was shipped off to India." She took a breath and declared, "Jules Stratford was strong and brave and kind and thoroughly capable of defending his country, his king, his troops, his family and himself."

"Tell me more."

Desiree searched her memory. "He loved soldiering, India, my great-grandmother, the Stratford, tea and me—not necessarily in that order. He loved to read and he loved to quote from the books he read." She glanced up at Mathis. "I believe you can tell a great deal about someone if you discover what books they read, don't you?"

His answer was terse. "Yes." Then he inquired, "What were some of the Colonel's favorite quotes?"

Desiree was a little reluctant to tell him. Her childhood memories of her great-grandfather were very personal and very precious to her. But she was also a reasonable woman. She knew Mathis Hazard wasn't asking out of some kind of perverse curiosity. He was trying to find difficult answers to difficult questions.

"He always told me to 'look to the stars.'"

"What do you think he meant by that?"

"I know what he meant. He was telling me that I could be whatever I wanted to be in life, that I could accomplish whatever I set my heart and mind to accomplish."

"Have you?"

"For the most part."

"What else?"

"My great-grandfather had a prodigious capacity to remember what he'd read. He often recited passages from the Bible, especially verses from the Book of Matthew."

"Do you recall what they were?"

Desiree was skeptical. "Do you honestly believe this is going to help?"

"I don't know what is going to help," Mathis said. "That's why I'm asking questions."

She crossed to a glass-fronted bookcase and carefully removed her great-grandfather's Bible. Jules Christian Stratford's favorite passages were marked with lengths of satin ribbon embroidered and given to him by her great-grandmother.

Desiree opened to one spot and read aloud. "'If thou wilt be perfect, go and sell what thou hast, and give it to the poor, and thou shalt have treasure in heaven.' Matthew 19:21." She went on to another. "'For where your treasure is, there will your heart be also.' Matthew 6:21. 'If therefore the light that is in thee be darkness, how great is that darkness.' Matthew 6:23." She raised her head. "My great-grandfather often quoted that particular verse to me when I was a young girl because he knew I was afraid of the dark."

"Are you still?"

"Am I still what?"

"Afraid of the dark?"

"No. Thankfully I outgrew that fear."

"Do you have others?"

He was getting rather too personal. Instead of answering his question, she asked one of her own. "We're all afraid of something, aren't we?"

He dodged the issue. "I suppose so."

She wasn't going to let him off the hook that easily. "What are you afraid of, Mathis Hazard?"

He hesitated for a moment, then said, "This isn't about me. It's about you."

Desiree closed the Bible and returned it to the bookcase. "My great-grandfather's favorite verse is also found in the Gospel of Matthew." She knew it by heart. "'Lay not up for yourselves treasures upon earth, where moth and rust doth corrupt, and where thieves break through and steal: But lay up for yourselves treasures in heaven.' ''

"Do you know why it was his favorite?"

"Does there have to be a reason?"

He shook his head. "But there could be one."

"I'm not aware of any reason." Her answer was inconclusive, but it was the best she could do. "The verse is a lot of people's favorite."

"Can you think of anything else?"

"Well, he used to tell me stories about his days in India. I loved them as a child. As an adult I recognize they were pretty far-fetched. He must have exaggerated the truth or perhaps he even made them up."

"Do you remember any of his stories?"

Desiree crossed to the row of windows. The morning light was streaming in through a crack in the draperies. She closed her eyes for a moment and felt the warmth of the sun on her face. "He used to describe traveling on the railroad—the intense heat, the hordes of people, the incredible spaces and the unfathomable mysteries that were India."

"I've never been to India," he said.

"Neither have I," she responded.

"Go on."

"Every year during the hot season, he and my great-grandmother would pack up their children, their servants, themselves and sometimes their entire circle of friends and journey up into the cooler mountain regions. They would stay in a vast stone house that had great bamboo fans suspended from the ceilings. The fans were operated by local children at the salary of fifty paisa per week. My great-grandparents and their friends would sit on a shaded veranda every afternoon and drink tea and discuss the state of the Empire. 'It was a time and place that will not come again, Desiree,' my great-grandfather used to say to me."

"The Colonel was right."

"Yes, he was." Desiree gave herself a shake. "There were dozens of stories, perhaps hundreds of stories, told to me when I was a child. I couldn't begin to relate all of them to you. But I recall that my great-grandfather once told me that he had been rewarded for saving a maharajah's son."

"What was the reward?"

Remembering, Desiree smiled. "I was very impressed that one of the gifts from the maharajah had been a real elephant. I was crushed to hear that it had been left behind in India when my great-grandparents emigrated to this country." She laughed a little self-consciously. "I remember wishing I had an elephant of my own." She sighed. "This isn't getting us very far, is it?"

The man never gave up. "I know Colonel Stratford has been gone for twenty years, but what about his personal papers?"

She indicated the desk drawers and bookcases. "They're still here. I've been going through them for several hours every night, as a matter of fact."

"Anything of interest?"

"Only to historians of Anglo-India and the Raj.

My great-grandfather kept letters, journals, you name it. It will take an archivist to go through it all.''

''Aren't documents your specialty?''

''I'm certainly qualified to evaluate and deal with historic papers.'' Now Desiree was speaking about one of her favorite topics. ''The problem is the high-acid paper introduced since the late nineteenth century. Many historic documents are disintegrating almost before our eyes. Hundreds of millions of one-of-a-kind documents will be unreadable in ten years.''

''It's the paper,'' Mathis concluded.

Desiree nodded. ''There are books made in 1100 that are in perfect condition. Quality paper can last indefinitely. Unfortunately cheap, high-acid paper was used, often as a wartime austerity measure, and now the acid is eating the cellulose fibers, causing the paper to fall apart. The trick is to neutralize the acids without dissolving the ink or damaging the bindings.''

''It's a race against time.''

''We're rushing to put deteriorating documents on microfilm, but millions of pages of history are likely to crumble away first,'' she said with her usual impassioned feelings for her work.

He had thought she was cold and heartless and without passion.

He had been wrong.

The woman was all cool, blond, good looks on the outside and a hot, bright red flame on the inside. Her name meant desire. Perhaps she was well named, after all.

Mathis watched her and found himself interested in learning more than he had ever dreamed possible about the lady from Boston. Maybe Beano was wrong. Maybe some women, some few women, weren't more trouble than they were worth. Maybe for each man there was one woman, and maybe that woman was worth the trouble.

Mathis was contemplating the irony of the situation in which he found himself when he started to get that feeling. It was a feeling he knew all too well from the old days. It was a feeling of wariness, of warning, a sensation of being watched.

He willed himself not to stiffen or give himself away by a change in his body language. Whoever was there—and he was damned certain someone was there—must not even guess that Mathis was aware of his presence.

But where was he…or she?

He let Desiree ramble on a little longer about the challenges of preserving documents. Meanwhile, he made a pretense of straightening several items on the desk—a brass inkwell, a green-shaded reading lamp, a photograph of a tall, elderly, distinguished-looking gentleman and a towheaded young girl; no doubt the Colonel and Desiree.

He glanced casually over his shoulder in the opposite direction from where the feeling was coming from. He studied their reflections in the glass-fronted barrister bookcases. He caught a glimpse of the adjoining door with the formal parlor. It was wide-open and no one was visible in the room next door. Nothing seemed out of place or amiss.

Mathis knew himself too well. He didn't get this feeling for no reason. It had saved his life and the lives of others on too many occasions. Some few people who knew them well claimed that it was a trait that seemed to run in the Hazard family.

He was about to dismiss the feeling of apprehension, anyway, when he heard a muffled sound nearby. It wasn't him and it wasn't Desiree. So who was making the noise?

Mathis stepped around the desk and put his mouth next to Desiree's ear. "Do exactly as I tell you," he whispered, nuzzling her neck.

His urgency conveyed itself to her. She looked up into his eyes and hers were suddenly wide with apprehension.

He slipped an arm around her waist and brought his lips to within a fraction of an inch of hers. "Kiss me."

Desiree opened her mouth and closed it again without saying a word.

"Now," he urged.

So Desiree Stratford went up on her tiptoes, wrapped her arms around his neck and kissed him.

Six

"'Stormy, husky, brawling, city of the big shoulders.'" That was what the poet Carl Sandburg had written about Chicago.

Desiree would have used the identical adjectives to describe Mathis Hazard. He had that same raw energy about him, that same law-unto-himself mentality, the same edge of roughness as the Windy City had had in the early years of its history.

Cattle and cowboys. Blazing guns and gangsters. Chicago had been the wild, Wild West in the Midwest. Neither the city nor the man would ever be truly civilized in Desiree's estimation.

But it wasn't uncivilized behavior, or even an impulsive act, that had driven Mathis Hazard to order her to kiss him. Desiree had sensed a subtle yet distinct change in him several seconds *before* he had slipped an arm around her waist and whispered urgently in her ear. Gradually she had become aware that he was listening, watching, searching for someone.

That someone was *not* her.

Then who was Mathis looking for? There was no one in this wing of the hotel except the two of them.

She had to trust him, Desiree reminded herself. This was someone who had the instincts of both man and beast. It would take somebody with those kind of gut-level abilities and a level head to go into the security business in the first place.

Besides, Mathis had made it clear that he was the boss. His orders were always given for a good reason. His orders were never issued frivolously. His orders could save her life and maybe even his own. She wasn't to question his orders or she might get them both killed…or at the very least injured.

So she kissed him.

In those first few moments Desiree was acutely aware that they were two strangers locked in an embrace, that they were a man and a woman feigning a passion that they couldn't possibly feel.

She quickly discovered, however, that it was a fine line between fantasy and reality. They were pretending passion existed between them. They were behaving in a passionate manner. It was a short leap to actually *feeling* passion.

She was warm, yet she was shivering. It was merely an act, only a ruse, nevertheless her heart was picking up speed. It didn't mean a thing. It couldn't mean anything. It wasn't real.

Their first kiss in the lobby had come and gone so quickly that she wasn't really familiar with the shape of this man's mouth. She didn't know whether his lips were large or small, thin or full. She couldn't recall if his skin was smooth or rough. She didn't recognize his smell or his taste or the feel of him beneath her hands.

Still, the unfamiliar could quickly become the familiar when two people were thrown together in an intimate situation.

Desiree breathed in deeply. Mathis smelled of natural things—the great outdoors, well-worked leather and well-washed cotton, and the clean scent of soap. Not a highly perfumed commercial soap, but one with the slightest hint of pine to it.

His taste was a heady mixture of fresh air and wide-open spaces, something faintly citrus and something she couldn't quite put her finger on. Perhaps it was the lingering flavor of a rich, dark coffee he'd drunk at breakfast.

Beneath her fingertips, his shoulders and arms and chest were hard and muscular, broad and strong. There didn't seem to be a spare ounce of flesh on his body.

This was a man without artifice. He was as straightforward as his kiss. He was direct. He was honest and honorable. He was a man of his word. He was a man who would never lie to a woman. All of this Desiree comprehended in the space of a minute, perhaps two. Then the realization hit her. She was kissing a complete stranger and enjoying it, savoring it, loving it!

Nonsense! She couldn't be. She didn't know the first thing about this man.

Well, she knew the first thing…or two…or three. Mathis Hazard was a wonderful kisser, a great kisser, even when his attention was focused on something else.

He was one of those men who could convey passion, curiosity, desire, intensity and incredible sensuality with a touch of his lips, the caress of his hand on her hair, the merest suggestion of a sigh that said he wasn't entirely acting the part of a lover.

Was Mathis having the same wild, irrational daydreams about her as she was about him?

It seemed highly unlikely. After all, he was using the kiss between them, and the embrace they were sharing, as camouflage.

Desiree felt the warmth of his breath waft across her face like a soft summer breeze off the lake.

More's the pity.

The danger had passed.

Mathis immediately corrected himself. The initial danger had passed; another type of danger was still very much in existence. In fact, he was holding it, *her,* in his arms.

He'd ordered Desiree to kiss him as a diversionary tactic for whoever might be listening or watching. It wouldn't be the first time, however, that a plan had started out as one thing and evolved into another.

The sensation of being watched had vanished into thin air. Here one minute, gone the next.

Desiree remained. Desiree with skin of porcelain and hair of silk. Desiree with lips of sweet honey and even sweeter wine. Desiree with a body that trembled in his arms.

Did she realize that she was trembling?

It had been fake. It became real. Suddenly Mathis was kissing her in earnest, not because he had to but because he wanted to, because he *needed* to.

He raised his head for a moment and gazed down into the face of the beautiful woman in his arms.

Her eyes fluttered open. "Mathis?"

He said it all when he murmured her name. "Desiree."

Then Mathis lowered his head and kissed her again, completely, thoroughly, utterly, to within an inch of her life. The thought briefly registered somewhere in the far recesses of his brain that it probably wasn't the smartest thing he had ever done.

He didn't care if it was dumb, Mathis realized. This time he was kissing her for himself.

Desiree was cool and she was burning hot. She was reluctant and she was eager. She was shy and she was bold, impassioned by what was taking place between them. She was drawing closer and pulling away. She wanted to kiss him and she was astonished that she was doing so. The woman was a mass of contradictions.

What woman wasn't?

He'd found himself in more than a few tight places in his thirty-six years, Mathis acknowledged. There had been more times than he cared to recall when it was real iffy whether he was going to get out alive. But he'd never deliberately walked into a trap. He'd never gotten in over his head when he had gone into a situation with his eyes wide-open…like his eyes were right now.

She wasn't his type.

Hell, he didn't even have a type. But in his guts he knew that it wasn't a woman—a lady—like Desiree Stratford. She was all pearls and Italian leather pumps. He was cowboy boots and a Stetson. She was East Coast. He was the wide-open spaces of New Mexico. She was a city woman. He was a man who needed to be away from it all in the country. She was a Boston Brahmin. He was the wild, Wild West.

Yet he didn't care how far apart their worlds were as long as he could kiss her, as long as he could have his hands on her, as long as she kissed him back as she was right now with her lips parted, her tongue titillated and titillating, her breath sweet, oh so sweet, and her body pressed tightly against his.

There was no doubt about it. The lady was enjoying herself. And so was he.

Mathis gave a low grumble of objection when Desiree finally pulled away and looked up at him.

"I believe the danger has passed," she announced a little breathlessly.

"Do you?"

Her eyes were a dark and mysterious shade of green. She swallowed with some difficulty and nodded.

That feeling was gone, but another and even stronger one had taken its place, and they both knew it.

Mathis dropped his voice to a confidential level. "Yes. The danger has passed."

Desiree took a step backward, straightened her suit jacket and patted at her chignon. "What was it?"

He was being completely honest with her when he admitted, "I don't know for sure."

She got a curious expression on her face. "I felt it."

"So did I."

Mathis spotted his white hat on the floor of the study. Sometime during their "scuffle" he had apparently dropped his Stetson. He bent over, retrieved the expensive hat and proceeded to brush the brim with the back of his hand.

Desiree went on. "I had the strangest sensation that someone was listening to us or even watching us."

"Me, too."

Her eyes darkened once more. "I couldn't tell where it was coming from."

Fifteen or twenty seconds elapsed before Mathis confessed to her, "I could."

Her mouth opened. "Where?"

"There," he said, indicating the wall behind her.

Desiree turned her head and stared at the study wall. "*There* is a wall," she said, stating the obvious.

"I know."

She wrinkled her brow into a frown. "That doesn't make sense, does it?"

Hell, no, it didn't make sense. But he had learned to trust his gut instincts. They were rarely wrong. Of course, his gut instincts had warned him about Desiree and he had refused to listen.

It was back to business.

"Where do we go from here?" Desiree inquired.

"I want your permission to make a complete inspection of the family living quarters."

"You have my permission," she said.

"I'd like to keep the note," he added.

She shrugged her shoulders and handed him the piece of vellum. "If you think it will be of any help."

"I'll also be making some discreet inquiries."

Blond eyebrows arched above intelligent green eyes. "With the emphasis on discreet, I hope."

"Of course." He could be as discreet as the next man. "I'll also need any architectural drawings of the hotel that you might have access to."

"I'm meeting with a team of architects this afternoon on possible renovation ideas. I'll see what I get from them," she offered.

"Thank you."

"Is there anything else you need?"

"A room for Beano."

"I'll have Mr. Modi see to it immediately." Desiree licked her lips. "And one for you, as well."

"I have a room."

Her head came around. "You do?"

Mathis nodded and steeled himself for the barrage of objections that was certain to follow his next announcement. "I'll be in the guest room next to your bedroom."

There was a moment of silence, then a quiet and ladylike "I see."

Did she see?

"It's necessary for your personal safety, Desiree."

Her eyes clouded over.

"'It is better to be prepared and have a strategic plan than to simply react to a situation,'" Mathis quoted again.

That brought a smile to her face. "The General, right?"

"The General."

"I must read 'The Art of War' sometime."

"I'll loan you my copy."

Desiree straightened her back. "Perhaps once this business is settled."

He couldn't blame her for not grabbing at the opportunity. "The Art of War" wasn't exactly bedtime reading.

Another thought occurred to Mathis some ten minutes later as he punched the button for the elevator. Someone had once written that "all's fair in love and war," but he was pretty sure it hadn't been General Sun Tzu.

Seven

He was no voyeur.

He might be many things—an eavesdropper, a fraud, a cheat, a liar, a thief, a weakling, sometimes a coward, certainly a fool, and *there was no fool like an old fool, as Charlotte used to say*—but he didn't like to think of himself as depraved, as a pervert, as a man who enjoyed watching others engage in private and intimate acts. So, once they started kissing each other, he turned his head and slipped away.

He was not a scoundrel. Indeed, there had been a time in his life when he had proudly called himself an officer and a gentleman. For that was what he had been.

But that was a long time ago, he reminded himself.

Nevertheless, the simple act of recalling his illustrious past made him straighten his stooped shoulders and stand a little taller, at least as much as the narrow passageway permitted.

He often lived in the past. The past was highly preferable to the present reduced circumstances in which he found himself. He stubbornly refused to consider the future, for that would be far too painful and self-defeating.

So it was more and more often into the past where he went and happily spent his time. In those days, those "glory days," a man had truly been a man. He had known where his place was in the world. He had been certain of who and what he was. He had been looked up to. He had been respected. He had been treated with dignity and honor. He had been hailed as a hero by one and all.

Glory days, indeed.

He reached up and wiped the back of his hand across his wrinkled cheek. "Old fool," he grumbled, encountering dampness.

There must be a leak dripping on him from somewhere overhead. The dampness on his face couldn't be tears. He wasn't crying. He never cried. As a matter of fact, he had never shed a tear in his life, not even last winter when Charlotte had died.

He took a handkerchief from his back pocket and dabbed at his eyes and nose. It must be allergies. Dust. Mold. Spores. And God alone knows what.

Allergies. That's what it must be.

He was not the villain, he told himself. He wasn't the one who had left that note on the desk with the dagger plunged through it. He wouldn't harm anyone. He wasn't out to hurt anyone or even to frighten them. That wasn't his intent at all.

He was simply looking after himself, and the ladies, of course. He was doing the noble thing, the selfless thing, the right thing. They deserved a roof over their heads.

No one liked change, least of all him. They, whoever *they* were, said that change was inevitable, but he didn't subscribe to that theory. Things did not have to change. Things could remain the same. The only inevitabilities were taxes and death, and a clever man could avoid the former if not the latter.

Survival. That's what this was all about. Surely a man had a right to fight for his own survival. Wasn't survival one of the basic human needs and rights?

It was his inalienable right to survive.

Liar!

He had sometimes been forced by circumstances beyond his control to lie to others. He had always vowed not to tell lies to himself. But he was now. The truth was that the only thing standing between him and the others was his infernal pride.

"Pride goeth before destruction, and an haughty spirit before a fall," according to Proverbs.

Well, he had fallen—oh, how far he had fallen!—but his pride, his blessed pride, his hellish pride, was intact. They all thought he had gone to a better place. His foolish pride would not permit him to let them know otherwise.

But he was surviving.

He moved like a ghost.

No one saw him.

No one heard him.

Well, not when he was careful. Every now and then, especially when he was tired or hungry, he had a tendency to grow a bit clumsy. Then he feared that someone had heard him, perhaps had even caught a glimpse of him.

But no one knew for certain that he was there.

They spoke of the age of the Stratford, of creaking floorboards, of the lack of insulation, of repairs and renovations that were desperately needed, of mice and—heaven forbid—even of rats, and sometimes they spoke of ghosts.

He didn't believe in ghosts. Not those kind, anyway. But there was something, someone, afoot.

He didn't have all the answers. He didn't know who had left the note of warning on old Jules's desk with the fancy dagger piercing it. He didn't know who was moving the furniture. Well, he had helped himself to a comfort or two, but it wasn't all his doing.

There was someone else who lurked in the shadows and sneaked about in the dead of the night.

Someone up to no good.

He would be the eyes and the ears and the heart of the Stratford, herself. He would look after her, protect her and keep her safe, as he had done for so many years.

The cowboy was right.

This was war.

Eight

"And it's rumored that on the anniversary of their deaths they wander the corridors of the Stratford, dodging phantom bullets and firing phantom tommy guns," Miss Maggie Mays was recounting to Mathis with particular relish when Desiree walked into the sitting room just off the main lobby.

Mathis realized that he had been watching for Desiree for the past quarter hour. It was twenty minutes after the Hotel Stratford's usual time for serving afternoon tea and it wasn't like her to be late. She was a punctilious and a punctual woman, as he had learned over the past several days.

"My apologies," Desiree extended to all present, settling in the only empty chair around the tea table. "I'm afraid I got caught up in a discussion with the art conservators over the best method for cleaning the mural in the lobby.'' She only hesitated briefly before adding, ''I hope you haven't waited tea for me.''

''We haven't, my dear,'' Miss Molly informed her. ''However, we saved a slice of carrot cake for you. We know how much you favor carrot cake.''

On the contrary, Mathis knew that Desiree never ate carrot cake. In fact, she couldn't abide carrot cake. From what he could gather, it had something to do with her general dislike of raisins.

Miss Maggie Mays was quick to admonish her twin. ''It's not Miss Stratford—'' The octogenarian came to an abrupt halt, cleared her throat, took a sip of tea and began again. ''It's not Mrs. Hazard who favors carrot cake, my dear.''

The other elderly woman was taken aback. She peered at her sibling over the rim of her spectacles. ''It isn't?''

Her sister shook her head.

A myopic gaze scanned those gathered around the tea table. ''Who is it, then?'' Miss Molly Mays finally inquired, perplexed by what she apparently considered to be an unexpected turn of events.

''Who *was* it?'' corrected Miss Maggie.

''Who *was* it?'' repeated Miss Molly.

Miss Maggie drew herself up and proclaimed, ''The Major.''

''Of course. How could I be so foolish as to confuse the two?'' The apologetic woman spoke directly to Desiree. ''I'm so sorry, Mrs. Hazard. I was thinking of someone else, of course. Your favorite is lemon cake, isn't it?'' She examined the assortment of delicacies on the tea tray. ''I'm afraid Andre isn't serving lemon cake today.''

''It's quite all right, Miss Mays. I'm not in the least bit hungry. I'll just have a cup of tea.''

''Shall I continue to pour?'' inquired the other sister.

''Please do,'' urged Desiree. ''And please continue with your conversation.''

''I was just remarking to Mathis that the Chicago City Council has issued a resolution exonerating Mrs. O'Leary and her cow, Daisy, in the touching off of the Great Fire of 1871,'' Miss Molly stated.

Miss Maggie was all ears. ''You don't say.''

''I do say.''

Her twin shook her head and made a particular kind of sound with her teeth. ''My, my, to be found innocent after all this time.''

''The City Council stated that the purpose of their resolution was not to lay blame elsewhere but to redeem history's mistreatment of a hardworking widow and her long-embattled cow.'' Miss Molly bent over at the waist, extended her head and neck rather like a pecking and clucking chicken, and confided in a stage whisper, ''It seems likely that the true culprit was one Daniel Sullivan, who was in Kate O'Leary's barn at the time.''

Miss Maggie sniffed, touched a dainty handkerchief embellished with pink crochet work to her nose and stated, ''While that may be all very well and good, sister, that was not what we were talking about.''

''It wasn't?''

''No, it wasn't. We were discussing the Major and his preference for carrot cake.''

Actually the old dears had been regaling him with ghost stories, but Mathis had heard quite enough for one afternoon about tortured spirits and other things that went bump in the night. And his curiosity about the Great Chicago Fire had certainly been more than satisfied. It was time to redirect the conversation.

He sat back as comfortably as he could in the uncomfortable chair. ''The Major?''

All three of the hotel's resident spinsters nodded their heads.

''Major Bunk,'' Miss Pye enlightened him. ''He was a longtime resident of the Stratford.''

''He's been gone nearly a year now,'' said one of the twins with a sigh.

''Passed on, has he?'' piped up Beano, who appeared almost as uncomfortable as Mathis as he attempted to balance a wafer-thin teacup on one knee and a Stetson on the other.

The Miss Mays beside Beano was quick to dissuade him of that impression. ''Oh, no, Mr. Jones, the Major didn't die. He was collected by his niece and her husband. He has gone to live with them in the country.''

''Lake Forest,'' volunteered her twin.

Mathis bit the inside of his mouth against a smile. ''I see.''

"We still hear from him once in a while, but not as often as we would like," said Miss Molly.

He was politely curious. "When was the last time the Major sent a note?"

This was apparently going to take some thought on the part of all three women.

"Well, we received a Christmas card from him. Remember, sister, it was a pretty thing with the nativity pictured on the front," recalled Miss Maggie.

"I remember," claimed the other.

"Then there was that lovely note he sent when Charlotte died," Cherry Pye reminded them.

"Indeed," the twins said in unison.

Miss Pye turned to the older man beside her. "I believe the last we heard from Major Bunk was this past February."

There was a sigh from an elderly Miss Mays. "The Major loved his tea."

The exchange between the twin sisters continued.

"And his tea cakes."

"He is sorely missed."

"It was nice to have a man about the place."

"Not as much trouble as we thought it would be."

"No, indeed."

A guileless smile appeared on a wrinkled face. "That's why it's so lovely having you two show up on our doorstep. We hope you gentlemen aren't planning to leave soon."

"Our plans are somewhat indefinite," Mathis said, giving no particular implication by his answer.

The Miss Mays were a study in pink today with

their rosy pink cheeks, pale pink skin and small, nondescript dark pink flowers scattered across the material of their pink dresses. There were even pink barrettes in their snowy-white hair. Mathis wondered if they had a sartorial consultation before dressing each morning.

Miss Maggie turned her pink-and-white head. ''What is your favorite tea cake, Mathis?''

He tried not to grasp the handle of his teacup too tightly for fear the delicate china would shatter in his hands. ''Tea cake?'' Since there was no way around it, he might as well come clean. ''I don't usually take tea,'' he confessed.

''You don't take tea?'' The thought had obviously never occurred to either of the Miss Mays. Although it was Miss Maggie who had inquired, they were both equally astonished by his answer.

''Why ever not?'' inquired Miss Molly.

Keep it simple, Hazard. Keep it truthful. ''I live and work on a large ranch. I'm usually out in the fields with the hired hands, or in one of the barns seeing to the livestock or in my office at this time of the afternoon,'' he stated.

''Sometimes I send a thermos of strong, black coffee out to him,'' Beano volunteered. ''And if he's lucky, a slice of my homemade peach pie to tide him over.''

''Tide him over?''

Beano expounded. ''Until he rides in for supper.''

''You mean on a horse?''

Beano snorted. ''Three hundred and fifty horses usually. I was referring to his pickup truck.''

It was apparently a foreign concept to the elderly ladies present. ''Pickup truck?''

''Everybody drives pickup trucks in New Mexico,'' Mathis said for his part.

Cherry Pye seemed intrigued by the notion. She put her fork down, reached up to adjust the bright purple flower attached by hairpins to her coiffure and asked, ''Even the women?''

''Especially the women,'' Beano declared with his characteristic grin. ''A woman can't find a cowboy if she don't have a truck.''

Which no doubt explained where she had gone wrong with men in the past, Desiree thought to herself with a wry smile as she took another sip of tepid tea.

''What kind of ranch do you have, Mathis?'' inquired his nearest companion.

''We have a little bit of everything on the new Circle H, Miss Molly,'' he responded.

''The *new* Circle H?''

Desiree waited, along with the others, for his explanation.

It was almost immediately forthcoming. ''I was born and raised on the old Circle H. It was my grandfather's ranch up in Wyoming. As a matter of fact, that's where Beano started out on his illustrious career as the best cook west of the Mississippi.''

"That was a long time before you were born, boss," spoke up his sidekick.

Cherry Pye wiped at the corners of her mouth with a linen napkin. "Do you have cows on the new Circle H?"

Mathis was all politeness. "Yes, ma'am, we do. But we call them cattle."

Beano was more effusive. "We've got gold, black gold and gold on the hoof."

"I'm afraid I've lived in Chicago my entire life, Mr. Jones," Miss Cherry Pye declared, pleading ignorance. "You'll have to explain what that means."

"Happy to oblige." Beano seemed only too happy as well to set his teacup down on the table in front of him. "Gold is just what it sounds like—gold ore out of the ground. Black gold is oil. Gold on the hoof is cattle. We got some of each."

One of the twins spoke up. "Is that where you gentlemen got the gold nuggets on your…ties?"

"Yes, it is, Miss Mays. These were the first two chunks Mathis and I took from his mine."

Desiree was fascinated. Of course, as his almost ex-wife, she was supposed to know all about Mathis's ranch in New Mexico.

One of the very pink Miss Mays inquired of her, "Is the Circle H a large ranch?"

"Oh, yes, it's a very large ranch. The Circle H must be at least—" Desiree decided to wing it and picked a number out of the air "—five hundred acres."

Mathis laughed heartily. "You never did have a head for figures, did you, sugar pie?"

Desiree felt her face grow warm.

He turned to the elderly woman. "Desiree means that the ranch is fifty thousand acres, give or take a thousand."

Her mouth dropped open and her head swung around. "Why, that's huge, Mathis."

"Not by New Mexico standards, darlin'. As you know, everything is bigger out West." He turned to the group gathered for tea. "Desiree will always be a city woman at heart. Sometimes the wide-open spaces are too wide and too open for her."

Everything certainly was bigger out West, Desiree reflected, including Mathis Hazard's ego and heaven knows what else.

It was past time she had another talk with the man in private. There were obviously important facts about his life that he hadn't seen fit to share with her. He had some explaining to do if she wasn't to be caught making a silly mistake again.

Beano finally got Mathis alone later that afternoon. The older man urged him aside, glanced around the hotel lobby to make sure they couldn't be overheard and then muttered under his breath, "The lady's in trouble, boss."

Mathis deliberately kept his voice low. "I know. That's why we're here."

Beano shuffled his feet and declared, "I don't mean that kind of trouble."

The muscles in Mathis's back and neck tightened. "What kind of trouble, then?"

His companion gave a snort of disdain. "The lady's fancy French chef up and quit right after tea this afternoon. Apparently someone criticized last night's spinach soufflé. So the man threw down his apron and stomped out in a huff."

"After eating Andre's idea of so-called fine cuisine for the past four days it's not a moment too soon," Mathis remarked.

Beano lowered his voice another notch. "There's nobody around this place who can cook but me."

Mathis wasn't going to argue and he wasn't going to ask his friend to take over the kitchen duties. That was Beano's decision.

"I don't mind stepping in and helping out," the older man said. "But it's up to you, boss."

Mathis was adamant. "No. It's up to you."

Beano cast a meaningful glance at him. "I'd like to fix a couple of my specialties, especially one of my home-baked pies, for Miss Pye," he confessed with a grin.

Mathis opened his mouth. "Then you can offer your services to Desiree if you like."

"You like Miss Desiree, don't you?"

Mathis shoved his hands into his pockets. He didn't say anything for a full half minute. Then he nodded his head and said, breath whistling out between his teeth, "Yes. I like her."

It wasn't smart.

It wasn't practical.

It didn't make a damned bit of sense.

The truth was, he liked Desiree Stratford far more than he cared to admit even to himself. The woman was driving him crazy…but it was the good kind of crazy.

It was several days after William "Beano" Jones had taken over the kitchen duties at the Stratford before he cornered Mathis again. The residents had just finished eating a hearty Western-style breakfast of eggs, hash browns, inch-thick steaks and flapjacks drizzled with maple syrup. The part-time help was washing up. The two men met in the hallway between the kitchen and the dining room.

Beano went first. "We've got a problem, boss."

That was becoming a familiar phrase these days. "What kind of problem?" Mathis asked.

"The lamb chop kind," Beano answered.

Mathis took in and let out a deep breath before he said, "Would you like to explain that?"

"I'm missing two leftover lamb chops from last night's dinner," came the cryptic response.

Mathis knew better than to make light of Beano's observations. The older man was tough and intuitive, if untaught.

His cook continued with his account of peculiarities in the kitchen. "The night before last half a pot of beef stew disappeared. The night before that it was a veal cutlet."

Mathis reached his own conclusions. "Someone is systematically stealing food from the hotel larders."

Beano wiped his hands on the kitchen towel tied around his waist. "That's about the size of it."

Mathis crossed his arms and planted his feet. "And you don't think it's any of the residents."

Beano shook his head.

"What about the kitchen help?" he asked, employing the process of elimination.

Dark chocolate brown eyes were unblinking. "I've been watching them like a hawk."

Mathis voiced the thought on both of their minds. "So someone else is taking the food."

"That's the long and short of it, boss," Beano summarized. Then he remarked, "You don't seem surprised."

Mathis confessed to his friend and sidekick, "I'm not. I've had my suspicions. The missing food cinches it."

"Cinches what?"

"My theory."

"Care to tell me what your theory is?"

He'd been meaning to confide in Beano, anyway. There was no time like the present. "This whole business has been an inside job."

George Huxley had hit the nail on the head the first day. He'd claimed it was an inside job. The ambassador had no idea just how right he'd been.

Beano rubbed his hand back and forth along his chin. "What do we do now?"

"*We* don't do anything. I'll take care of the problem," Mathis guaranteed him.

"You know where to find me if you need me,"

the older man declared as he headed back to his domain.

"What's for dinner?" Mathis called after him.

"One of your least favorites," Beano answered.

"What's that?"

"Humble pie."

Nine

Beano had outdone himself.

Desiree would be the first to admit that the former chuck wagon cook was a far superior chef to the Stratford's recently departed French *cuisinier,* Andre.

This evening, dinner had been a succulent beef tenderloin stuffed with lobster, seasoned new potatoes grilled to a perfect golden brown and asparagus, served al dente, of course, and with a side of Beano's own special hollandaise sauce.

The Stratford's permanent guests were still sitting in the hotel dining room, sipping a cup of Beano's special coffee, lingering over a slice of Beano's special homemade pie, exclaiming about the change for the better in their culinary fortunes.

Desiree had suddenly had to escape. Informing

Mr. Modi, the trio of elderly ladies and Mathis that she required time to review renovation plans and costs and that she needed to sort through her great-grandfather's papers, she had excused herself immediately after dinner and retreated to the solitude of the upstairs study.

The truth was she had wanted time by herself, time to think, time to sort through her feelings, time to ponder the problem of Mathis Hazard.

The man was getting on her nerves. He was always poking his nose into her business, showing up wherever she happened to be in the hotel, wanting information, asking questions, keeping an eye on her.

The man rubbed her the wrong way. He was arrogant. He was bossy. He was dictatorial. He was too good-looking for his own good...and hers. He was too tall. He was too self-assured. He was far too perceptive. He was even too charming in a rustic sort of way. He was too much, period.

Then why couldn't she stop thinking about him?

"He isn't your type," Desiree stated aloud. "Besides, you're not attracted to him." After half a minute she exhaled on a long, drawn-out sigh. "Liar."

Okay, so maybe she was attracted to Mathis, but it was strictly a physical thing. It was nothing more than prurient interest, carnal attraction, plain, old sex.

Oh, boy, she was in even bigger trouble than she had imagined, Desiree realized. If she was honest with herself she had to admit that she hadn't felt this way since the teenage crush she'd had on Tommy Fielding back in high school.

Well, she wasn't in high school any longer. In fact, at the age of thirty, she was far from it. Nevertheless, men were not her strong suit. Frankly, they never had been and they never would be. The male of the species had always been something of a mystery to her. For their part, they seemed to find her both attractive and irritating. She couldn't understand why.

Perhaps she did know why. By nature, she was fastidious. She was discriminating, rather particular, perhaps even downright picky. Men had a tendency to think of her as cool, as cold, even as glacial, and all because she refused to fall into bed with everyone she consented to go out with on a date.

She wasn't going to start apologizing for what she was, Desiree decided.

She was what she was.

"What exactly is that?" Desiree queried herself. She answered her own question. "Intelligent. Well educated. Professionally successful. Not bad-looking. Perhaps even pretty. Decent figure." She frowned. "Unattached. Unmarried. Unloved."

She didn't care for the direction of her thoughts. Determined to put the subject of men and one man in particular from her mind, she curled up on the sofa and opened one of her great-grandfather's leather-covered journals that she had taken from the bookcase. On the title page, written in his own distinct hand, was *Jules Christian Stratford, 1929-1930, India.*

Desiree turned to a page marked by a brown satin ribbon and began to read.

April 5, 1929

Grace and I have received an invitation to visit the Maharajah at his summer palace. It is a singular honor. Sardar and Kamla will accompany us on the journey. The children will be left at home, of course, in the care of their ayahs.

April 23, 1929

The Maharajah has been a most gracious and welcoming host to Grace and myself. We have been given a suite of luxurious rooms in the palace, although nothing as lavish or spacious as what we have seen of the prince's own living quarters.

The prince has many treasure chambers. Among them is the *Tokshakhana* for men's and women's valuable clothing, the *Kawalkhana* for chandeliers, candelabra, crystal and Venetian glass and the *Jawarkhana* for family jewels and religious items studded with precious stones.

We have been presented with numerous gifts. For Grace, a *chadar,* or shawl, and a miniature painting of royal ladies reposing in a lush garden.

For myself, a *choga,* or a long, formal coat, heavily embroidered, and an antique tapestry depicting a long-ago hunt of one of the Maharajah's own ancestors. He tells me that two dozen tigers and eleven thousand grouse were bagged in a single day.

Tomorrow I will go hunting with the Maharajah, his eldest son and his courtiers. Grace will take tea with his wife, the Maharanee. We are both abundantly aware of the honor being bestowed on us.

April 28, 1929

It has been the most extraordinary week. I scarcely know where to begin to recount the events of the past few days. The day of the hunt we were not long on our way, perched atop our elephants, native beaters coming toward us through the jungle, driving the tigers in our direction, when we alighted from our mounts and prepared our guns.

What happened next is something of a blur in my mind. I must confess that I have found all the ensuing fuss quite disconcerting. But I digress.

In the hustle and bustle, I spotted something moving off to the rear of our hunting party. I felt a distinct chill despite the intense heat of the day. Then I realized it was a huge tiger and it was headed straight for the Maharajah's unprotected son.

I did what any gentleman and soldier would do. I had no time to think, only to act. Placing myself between the young prince and the attacking animal, I took aim and fired. It was a lucky shot. My first bullet caught the creature directly between the eyes. The tiger dropped dead at my feet.

The Maharajah has not stopped thanking me since. Last night a banquet was held in my honor and I was presented with my choice of elephants, one of the Maharajah's own prized Rolls-Royces and the fabled Bengal Lights. I was overwhelmed. I wanted to refuse, but there is nothing to be done but to politely accept the tributes.

I am thankful, of course, that I was able to save the young prince's life. But I shall never forget the wild beauty of the creature I was forced to kill.

I am reminded of the lines from the poem by William Blake. ''Tiger! Tiger! burning bright / In the forests of the night....In what distant deeps or skies / Burnt the fire of thine eyes?''

I have confided to Grace that I don't believe I shall ever go hunting again.

Desiree looked up from her great-grandfather's journal and stared, unseeing, across the study. Tears blurred her vision. Her throat was constricted with emotion. No wonder she had loved this man so very dearly. Jules Christian Stratford had been a gentleman in the truest sense of the word.

She managed a smile as she recalled her childhood disappointment upon discovering that the prized elephant had not been brought from India to Chicago with her great-grandparents.

Then Desiree frowned in puzzlement. She glanced

back down at the page and read in a whisper, "'I was presented with the fabled Bengal Lights.'"

What were the Bengal Lights?

Among all the stories and anecdotes and adventures that her great-grandfather had related to her during her childhood, Desiree was certain he had never mentioned the Bengal Lights. She could only assume that they hadn't been important.

Then why had Grandpapa referred to them in his journal as the *fabled* Bengal Lights?

Something, some sixth sense, some gut instinct, some feeling in the pit of her stomach, told Desiree that the Bengal Lights, whatever they were, were important.

What were they?

What could have happened to them?

She put the journal down, got up from the sofa and crossed to one of the glass-fronted bookcases. She took out a Webster's dictionary and thumbed through to the *B*s. "Bengal light, a blue light used formerly for signaling and illumination; or any of various colored lights or flares."

That wasn't much help.

She slammed the dictionary shut and grumbled under her breath, "Hell's bells."

"Tsk-tsk. Such language from a lady." The deep, sardonic male voice had come from the doorway.

Desiree spun around. "Mathis."

A small, mocking smile appeared on the man's lips. "Desiree."

"I, ah, was looking something up in the dictionary."

Mathis Hazard leaned nonchalantly against the door frame, one hand in the pocket of his jeans, the other braced against the jamb. Didn't the man ever wear anything but skintight blue jeans?

"You don't seem too pleased with whatever you found," he noted.

"That's the problem. I didn't find," she informed him.

A dark, nearly black eyebrow was arched in her direction. "What were you looking for?"

Desiree took in and let out a breath before she inquired, "You don't happen to know what the Bengal Lights are, do you?"

Mathis shook his head. "Sorry."

"Don't be." She replaced the dictionary. "Frankly I don't have a clue, either."

He hovered in the doorway.

She could take a hint. Besides, she'd been meaning to have a chat with him since the afternoon when she'd nearly put her foot in it about the size of his ranch. "Would you like to..."

Mathis moved with lightning speed. Before Desiree could complete her sentence he was making himself comfortable on the opposite end of the sofa from where she had been curled up.

"...join me?" she finished.

He flashed her a smile. "Thank you. I would."

Desiree found she was suddenly feeling rather self-conscious. She said the first thing that popped into her head. "I've been studying one of my great-grandfather's journals."

Mathis picked up the leather volume she had left on the sofa. *"Jules Christian Stratford, 1929-1930, India,"* he read aloud. Then he replaced the book and glanced up at her questioningly. "Have you discovered anything interesting?"

"Interesting, yes. Useful, no." Desiree resumed her seat, crossed one leg demurely over the other and smoothed the green silk shirt she'd changed into after dinner, along with a matching pair of green silk slacks. "I was reading the account of how my great-grandfather saved the maharajah's son from a tiger attack."

"An heroic deed surely worthy of an elephant or two as reward," Mathis ventured.

"And apparently a Rolls-Royce and something called the Bengal Lights."

"Ah." It was a very telling "ah."

"Yes, that's why I asked if you knew what the Bengal Lights are, or were," she confirmed.

"Do you think they're important?"

Desiree shrugged her silk-clad shoulders and confessed, "I don't know. My great-grandfather refers to them only as the *fabled* Bengal Lights." She decided to volley the ball back into his court. "How is your investigation going?"

This time it was Mathis who shrugged his shoulders. "It's a little premature to say."

"Have you discovered anything interesting?"

"Interesting, yes. Useful, I don't know," he answered guardedly, echoing her own claim. "I'd like to reserve judgment until I have a few more unanswered questions answered."

Apparently Mathis Hazard was a man who played his cards close to his chest.

Desiree brought up another subject. "By the way, I felt rather foolish getting caught like that at tea the other day," she informed him. "As your almost ex-wife surely I would know something more about your life than I do."

Mathis spread his arms and gave her one of his disarming smiles. "My life is an open book," he declared. Then he added, "What would you like to know?"

"What did you do before you decided to become a security expert for Hazards, Inc.?"

"A little of this. A little of that."

"Would you care to be more specific?"

"I had a variety of jobs."

She blew out her breath. "Let's start at the beginning. I believe you mentioned that you were born in Wyoming."

Mathis nodded.

She went on. "That's where you grew up."

"I lived on my grandfather's ranch from the time I was born until the age of nineteen."

"That would have been the old Circle H?"

He moved his head again.

"What about your parents?"

"I scarcely remember my mother. She died when I was just a kid. My father had trouble settling down after she was gone. He did everything from soldiering to law enforcement. It was my grandfather who raised me.''

''Your grandfather and Beano?''

''Yes.''

It was like pulling teeth to get Mathis to talk about himself. ''Go on,'' she urged, gesturing with her hand.

''I left my grandfather's ranch at the age of nineteen and enlisted in the army. Eventually I joined the Army Rangers. I went to college. I worked for the Border patrol. I did a few special assignments.'' Desiree noticed he didn't elaborate on for whom he did those special assignments, but she could guess. ''I occasionally do some work for my cousin, Jonathan Hazard, who owns and operates Hazards, Inc.''

'''Tinker, tailor, soldier, spy,''' Desiree murmured meaningfully.

There was a momentary hesitation, then the admission. ''Something like that.''

''Where does rancher fit into the list?''

She could see him relax. ''I'm semi-retired from the security business. Ranching is what I primarily do these days.''

''You have a very large ranch.''

He chuckled. It was a deep rumble in his chest. ''Somewhat larger than you apparently realized.''

''I almost gave the show away.''

Mathis was quick to reassure her. ''Don't worry. There isn't a suspicious bone in either of the Miss

Mays or Miss Pye. I'm sure they chalked it up to ignorance."

Her eyebrows rose a fraction of an inch. "Thanks."

"No offense intended."

"None taken."

If there had been a time for subtlety, Desiree decided it was long past. "I assume you've never been married?"

"You assume correctly." Intent masculine eyes looked directly into hers. "You've never been married."

She moved her head. "Do you have a significant other?"

"Nope." His eyes darkened. "There's no one special in your life, either."

Mathis seemed to know a great deal about her personal statistics. "Background check?"

He nodded. "And I had a long chat with George Huxley," he admitted.

"Uncle George talks too much."

Desiree noticed that Mathis didn't try to deny the charge. "George is very fond of you."

"And I'm very fond of him," she stated with a small sigh.

"His only concern is for your safety."

"That's why he hired you."

"That's why he hired me." There was a moment or two of silence. "I hope you feel safer with me sleeping next door."

The man had to be joking. "I do." Desiree's breath stuck in her throat. "And I don't."

It took him an instant to laugh. "Well, which is it?"

Desiree only hesitated briefly and said, "Both."

Mathis moved closer to her on the oversize, overstuffed sofa. "Do I make you nervous?"

She couldn't look away from his mouth. She moistened her lips and confessed, "Yes."

"Would it help if I told you that you make me feel the same way?" he said.

His question surprised her. She bit her bottom lip and nodded. "A little, I suppose." She didn't feel nonchalant when she asked, "Why do I make you nervous?"

Muscles in broad, masculine shoulders tightened. "Because I find myself attracted to you. I didn't expect to be. I don't want to be. It isn't smart. In fact, it's downright stupid on my part. This is business, and business and pleasure don't mix. It's an unwritten rule."

"Some people would say that rules are meant to be broken," Desiree alleged.

Mathis seemed to find her suggestion vaguely amusing. "I can't imagine that you're one of those people."

She wasn't under ordinary circumstances, but there was nothing ordinary about the man or the circumstances in which she presently found herself. "I'm not."

He evidently believed that turnaround was fair play. ''Why do I make you nervous?''

Desiree picked up her great-grandfather's journal, marked her place with the brown satin ribbon and placed it on the parson's table behind the sofa. Then she wrapped her arms around herself, as if they would somehow serve as protection. She finally met his dark-eyed gaze. ''I'm attracted to you, as well. I didn't expect to be. I certainly don't want to be, either. Ours is a business relationship. And I never mix business and pleasure.''

''But you're considering doing just that, aren't you?'' The man didn't mince words.

It was time to be honest with herself and with Mathis. Her voice was a husky murmur. ''Yes.''

''Damn, so am I,'' Mathis swore. He held out a hand toward her. Desiree slowly unfolded her arms, reached out and placed her hand in his. ''That wasn't so hard, was it?''

She shook her head.

''We're two mature and consenting adults, Desiree,'' he went on. ''We can take this as slow or as fast as we want. What we do and how far we go is entirely up to us.'' He gave her hand a reassuring squeeze. ''Anytime you want something, just ask. Anytime you want to stop, just say so. Agreed?''

She swallowed. ''Agreed.''

''I want to kiss you. Do you want to kiss me?''

She nodded.

He slowly drew her across the sofa and into his

arms. His fingers shifted to her face. ''You have the softest skin I've ever touched.''

She swallowed again, harder this time. ''I suppose you've touched a lot of women.''

''Not all that many. It's difficult to meet the right kind of women in my line of work.''

Desiree was curious. ''What is the right kind of woman?''

Ten

Was this one of those trick questions women always liked to ask men?

Mathis cleared his throat and racked his brain for an answer. "I suppose it's different for each man."

Huge jade-green eyes gazed directly into his. "I suppose it is."

Muscles in his back tightened again, but Mathis knew he had to go on. "The right kind of woman would be dependable, loyal, steadfast, a true and faithful companion." He realized that he had just described the golden retriever he'd had as a boy.

Desiree listened intently and made a small sound very much like "hmm" in the back of her throat.

She had a lovely throat and a lovely neck, for that matter. Her neck was long and graceful and pale ivory in color. It swept out on either side into flawless shoulders and down to the swell of what promised to be a pair of perfect breasts. Mathis almost blurted out that the right kind of woman would have perfect breasts, as well, but somehow he didn't think that was a politically correct answer.

He flexed his tense shoulders, quietly blew out his breath and said to her, "The right kind of woman would be intelligent, good-tempered, have a sense of humor and possess a certain generosity of spirit."

Desiree made the same small sound again. Was she agreeing or disagreeing with him?

Mathis consciously relaxed his shoulders and continued. "The right woman would be attractive."

A finely arched blond eyebrow was raised and lowered. "In other words, she would be beautiful."

Mathis shook his head. "She wouldn't necessarily have to be beautiful. I know it sounds like a cliché—" hell, that's because it was a cliché "—but beauty is only skin deep. When I think of an attractive woman, I think of the whole package—nice figure, nice hair, nice skin, nice voice, nice smell."

"Nice."

He nodded. "Nice."

Desiree appeared to be frowning. Had he missed something? Had he failed to mention something important?

Mathis took a moment and thought hard. Maybe it was his choice of words. Maybe he should have come up with a better description than *nice*.

"Nice can be an insipid word," he finally submitted.

"It can be," she allowed.

"I didn't mean it like that," he assured her.

"I'm sure you didn't."

"When I say nice what I really mean is congenial and—" he shrugged "—agreeable."

A dainty nose was wrinkled in what appeared to be mild distaste. "Agreeable."

Mathis suddenly realized that he was digging a damned nice hole for himself. The more he talked, the deeper the hole got. The trouble was he didn't want to talk to Desiree. What he wanted to do was kiss her. Kiss her and a whole lot more. But the woman wanted words, so he'd give her words.

He forged ahead. "The right woman is someone a man can trust with his life."

That statement seemed to grab Desiree's attention. Her expression came alive. "Trust is very important."

"Trust is rare between a man and a woman."

She raised her head a notch and looked intently at him. "Do you think so?"

Mathis knew so. Actually, trust was pretty darn scarce between any two people.

Desiree probed. "Who do you trust?"

"Beano."

"Of course."

"Jonathan."

"Your cousin."

He added, "Most of the Hazards."

"Your family."

Mathis moved his head in the affirmative and asked Desiree the same question. "Who do you trust?"

She moistened her lips. Lips that were only inches from his. Lips that enticed him. Lips that tempted him. Lips that, like a magnet, drew him closer and closer.

"I trust my parents, a few close friends, several of my colleagues at the museum and Uncle George, naturally."

"Naturally."

"I suppose in some ways you could say that I trust my doctor, my dentist, my lawyer, my stockbroker, my accountant, the woman who cleans my apartment."

"I suppose you could."

"I trust certain public figures." She quickly qualified her answer. "Of course, not politicians."

"Of course not."

Mathis felt himself growing impatient. There had been enough talk. It was time to take action. He closed the space between them, murmured her name and brought his mouth down on hers.

It was what he'd wanted to do for days. In fact, it was as though he'd been holding his breath since the first morning when they had kissed in this very room.

What made him want to kiss this woman and go on kissing her?

Mathis knew the answer to his own question. He wanted to kiss Desiree because she was delicious to look at, delicious to smell, delicious to taste, delicious to touch. It was as if she were everything that his senses found sensual, exciting, desirable.

He told himself it had nothing *and* everything to do with the fact that he was itching to get his hands on her. But his gut instincts warned him that he'd better use his head with this woman, not just his hands. If he revealed the depth of his desire for her too soon he might scare the lady off. That was the last thing he wanted to do.

Mathis started out with good intentions. He had intended to kiss Desiree softly, invitingly, enticingly. He had intended to brush his lips back and forth across hers, tasting her. He had intended to inhale deeply and then hold his breath for a moment and savor her scent.

Hell was paved with good intentions.

One minute he was kissing her, the next he was devouring her with his mouth, his lips, his teeth, his tongue. It had started out innocently enough when she had placed her hand in his. Somehow she ended up crushed to his chest with her arms wrapped around his neck.

One minute it was cool, calm and collected, the next it was hot and heavy and spiraling out of control.

Mathis realized somewhere in the back of his mind, which was the only part of his brain that still seemed to be functioning, that he was in danger of losing control of himself, of Desiree and certainly of the situation.

He should stop kissing her. He should firmly yet gently put her back on her side of the sofa. He should remember that he was here on business, not pleasure. And he definitely should know better.

He should *not* be contemplating which was silkier—Desiree's blouse or the skin underneath. He should *not* be picturing his hands on her shoulders, her waist, the softly rounded swell of her breasts. He certainly should *not* be imagining her without a stitch of clothing on, stretched out beneath him on the sofa, her legs wrapped around his thighs, her cries of ecstasy filling his mouth.

But Mathis didn't give a tinker's damn about what he should or shouldn't be doing. All he could think about was Desiree of the silky skin, Desiree of the lush and inviting body, Desiree of the impassioned kisses and the eager, caressing hands.

For she was caressing him, her fingertips flitting across his face like the soft beat of a butterfly's wings, her fingernails gripping his shoulders as if she were holding on for dear life, her hands taking full measure of his arms and chest and waist.

He wanted her hands on him: tousling his hair; tracing the outline of his ear, his jaw, his mouth; stroking his chest and unintentionally or, well, maybe not so unintentionally, brushing across his nipples; then lower to where his jeans rode on his hips, and lower still to the top of the metal zipper and finally to its base where his body strained against the denim material.

Mathis couldn't stop the groan of arousal that

slipped from between his lips. He was driving himself crazy. Desiree was driving him crazy. From that first day he had recognized on some instinctive level that she would be his undoing, his downfall, his waterloo. She would be the death of him yet.

But what a way for a man to go! He was burning up from the inside out, white-hot flames of desire licking, flicking, arousing every nerve ending in his body.

He couldn't, he wouldn't, lose all semblance of control. Years of specialized training, of always listening with one ear cocked, of always keeping an eye out, of never letting go completely, never trusting implicitly, never entrusting himself—and certainly not his heart—to another's care: they all stopped him now.

Mathis shivered and relaxed his hold on Desiree.

Drawing back an inch or two, she raised her chin and stared up into his eyes. She tried to speak but nothing came out. She tried again. "What is it, Mathis?"

He struggled to form an intelligible response. "Nothing."

She frowned. "Nothing?"

He immediately sought to reassure her. "It's not you."

The frown line between her eyes deepened. "If it's not me, then who is it?"

Mathis bit off an expletive. His hand instinctively went to the hair at the back of his neck. "Me."

Tension clung to Desiree's lovely features. She regarded him for some time. "I don't understand."

Neither did he.

"I don't think this is a great idea." He immediately backtracked. "Well, it's a great idea, but it's not a good idea." He took in a deep breath and slowly exhaled. "It's probably not a smart idea."

"Do you always do what's smart?"

Hell, no.

He shook his head. "Far from it." So why was he so dead set on playing it smart now?

Because Desiree wasn't the kind of woman a man took to bed and then waved goodbye to as he collected his hat and boots on the way out the door the next morning. Because she was the kind of woman a man cherished, appreciated, treasured, loved. Because she was the kind of woman a man married.

That's when it hit Mathis. *Because Desiree was the right kind of woman.*

She was still talking. "But tonight you're determined to do what you think is smart."

Mathis was feeling quite noble when he placed her on the opposite end of the sofa and sat back. "That's about the size of it."

Enigmatic green eyes watched him. "What if I don't want to do what is smart?"

That stopped him cold. Mathis ran his hand back and forth along his jawline, and heard the scrape of beard stubble against skin. "I have to admit the possibility never occurred to me."

Desiree tilted her head to one side and asked, "Why not?"

He could think of a thousand reasons. Okay, maybe that was an exaggeration, but he could certainly think of half a dozen. "I can think of at least half a dozen good reasons."

Desiree challenged him. "Name one."

"You aren't the impulsive type."

She cocked a brow. "Neither are you."

"Neither am I usually," he confirmed.

She went on to observe, "I assume it wouldn't have been smart in your line of work."

"It would have been downright stupid in my line of work," he confirmed.

Desiree folded her arms across her breasts. "Name another reason."

"You're a lady."

She was adamant. "I'm a woman."

"You're a woman and a lady." He kept going. "You're intelligent, well-bred and well educated, and you live by high moral standards."

A faint hint of color washed her cheeks. "Thank you." She passed her tongue over her lips. "I think."

"It was meant as a compliment, Desiree."

"Then that's how I'll choose to see it."

He could hear the injury in her voice. "As opposed to what?"

"Rejection."

Women! He would never understand women. He would certainly never understand this woman. Beano was right. You couldn't live with them and sometimes they were nothing but trouble!

Mathis threw up his arms and confessed, "This isn't going very well, is it?"

Desiree sat stiffly. Her posture was stiff, her expression was stiff, her bottom lip was stiff. "No, it isn't."

Mathis gave a short, humorless laugh. "Maybe I shouldn't have invited myself to join you tonight."

Her spine was ramrod straight against the back of the sofa. "Maybe you shouldn't have."

"I guess I should go."

"I guess you should."

Mathis got to his feet and walked toward the study door. He paused and considered, then shook his head slowly. "I would never intentionally hurt you, Desiree."

He saw her struggle for a response. "I know you wouldn't," she said in a husky voice.

"I'm here to do a job and I'm here to keep you safe." The reminder was for both their benefits.

A small acknowledgment was given in return. "I know."

Mathis shoved his hands into the front pockets of his jeans. "I'll say good-night, then."

It was several heartbeats later before she responded. "Good night, Mathis."

Sometimes there was a strong element of truth in a cliché, Mathis decided as he ambled down the hallway toward the guest bedroom. In his case it was certainly true. A man was damned if he did and damned if he didn't.

He was still half-aroused. He could still taste Desiree on his lips. He could still feel Desiree in his hands.

Mathis blew out his breath expressively. It was going to be a very long night.

Eleven

Desiree couldn't sleep.

She had tried poring over a tedious financial report. She had tried reading her great-grandfather's journal. She had tried experimenting with the technique of tensing and then relaxing one by one different muscles in her body. She had tried staring at the stars twinkling overhead in the mural on her bedroom ceiling. She had even tried counting sheep.

Nothing had worked.

It was in the wee, small hours of the night and once again she was wide-awake.

Desiree knew what the problem was. She was frustrated. She was hot and bothered. She had been sexually aroused and then left dissatisfied and unsatisfied. She couldn't remember the last time *that* had happened to her.

It was all Mathis Hazard's fault.

She immediately retracted her statement. It wasn't really Mathis's fault. He hadn't set out to kiss her, to excite her, to reduce her to a mass of quivering female flesh. Well, if he had, she'd certainly been a willing accomplice.

Desiree exhaled on a long, drawn-out sigh. He wasn't to blame. She wasn't to blame. No one was to blame. It was simply something that had happened between a man and a woman who were attracted to each other. It was something that happened thousands, even millions, of times every day between men and women.

Just not between her and a man.

Desiree punched at the pile of pillows behind her back. She was the kind of woman who always tried to do the correct thing, the proper thing, the right thing. But right for whom? That was the question. Was it the right thing for her parents? For her co-workers? For the museum? For the Stratford?

What was right for her?

What did she want?

Who did she want?

"Mathis," she said aloud.

Desiree's hand flew to her throat. Did she really want Mathis Hazard? How could she possibly want, desire, hunger for, perhaps *love* a man she had known for little more than a week?

Because when it came to a woman's heart, time was irrelevant, she reminded herself.

Was her heart involved? Did love enter into her feelings for Mathis? Did the emotion she was experiencing run deep like a dark, swift-coursing river? Or was it superficial and shallow? Perhaps nothing more than infatuation or plain, old-fashioned lust?

Mathis Hazard was *nothing* that she had thought she wanted in a man, and yet it turned out that he was *everything* she had ever dreamed of.

Yes, he was rough around the edges. Yes, he was tough and stubborn and uncompromising, and, yes, sometimes trying to reason with him was like hitting her head against a brick wall.

Yet he was also tall, dark and exceedingly handsome. He had intelligent eyes, a quick and perceptive mind, a disarming smile and the best body she had ever seen on a man...clothed, anyway. She couldn't speak for his body without clothes.

But she'd like to.

Desiree sighed and continued with her evaluation. Mathis was strong in body, mind and spirit. He was a gentleman in the truest sense of the word, much like her great-grandfather had been. Mathis would always look after his own: his own country, his own integrity, his own honor, his own promises and commitments, his own family, his own wife.

Wife.

There was that word again. Due to the scheme cooked up by George Huxley and Mathis, she had unwillingly and unwittingly been cast in the role of

Mathis's wife. In the beginning, it had seemed strange to be referred to as Mrs. Hazard by the Stratford's resident guests. Even the manager, Mr. Modi, now called her by her married name.

Desiree caught herself. She had no married name. She wasn't married to Mathis Hazard or to anyone else for that matter. She was unmarried. She was unattached. She was a single woman. She was what society used to call an old maid.

Desiree gave the Egyptian cotton pillows another forceful punch with her fist.

Great! That certainly lifted her spirits. First, the most attractive man she'd ever known—and the man she was the most attracted to—had left her high and dry. Then she seemed doomed to lie awake half the night with a full-blown case of insomnia, and now she had to face the fact that she was an old maid.

If she was a drinking woman, she would get up and help herself to a brandy from the liquor cabinet in the study. But she had never thought it a good idea for a woman to drink alone.

Of course, there was always the time-honored remedy of a glass of warm milk. She hadn't tried that particular cure for sleeplessness since she was a very little girl.

Desiree had a vague recollection of her great-grandmother—the memory was no more than a shadowy impression of a gentle woman with silvery hair, ivory skin, a soft voice, and the lingering scent of lilac toilet water—bringing her a glass of warm milk in this very room, when she was five or six.

Indeed, it was one of her few remaining memories of her great-grandmother, although her great-grandfather had spoken of his beloved Grace until the day he'd died.

Until death us do part.

Was that kind of love still possible between a man and a woman in a world where everyone and everything seemed so easily and readily disposed of? Could it be the reason she had chosen never to marry? Was it because she wanted the everlasting kind of love, the evermore kind of love, forever love?

Pondering one of life's great imponderables wasn't going to help her get to sleep, Desiree acknowledged.

"Then how about a medicinal glass of milk?" she asked herself out loud.

In one swift movement she threw back the covers, switched on the reading lamp beside the bed, reached for the jade-green silk bathrobe that matched the jade-green silk pajamas she was wearing and slid her feet into a pair of slippers.

Desiree opened the door to her bedroom and glanced back toward the other guest room for a moment. Was that a light she saw under the door? Was Mathis still awake as well? She started down the hallway toward the elevator.

The trip downstairs to the hotel's kitchen took a good ten minutes, but it seemed longer. Desiree tried to convince herself that the snail's pace of the original elevator added to the Stratford's historic charm, but she knew it wasn't true. At least not in the dead of night, and not when she was all alone.

Once she reached the kitchen it took her another ten minutes to gather the necessary utensils, pour the milk into a saucepan and heat it on the stove top. The idea of warming a glass of milk in the microwave oven didn't appeal to her. Tonight she wanted to do it her great-grandmother's way.

Nevertheless, she found herself tapping her foot with impatience before it was all said and done.

Desiree had never noticed how many nooks and crannies and dark, shadowy corners there were in the hotel's kitchen. Every sound seemed magnified in the middle of the night. The clatter of the copper saucepan as she took it from the rack overhead. The sound of the spoon, metal scraping against metal, as she occasionally stirred the milk. Even the soft gurgle as she poured it from the pan into a large glass.

She took a sip.

The warm milk didn't seem to have her great-grandmother's magical touch to it, but it would have to do.

Making sure she had turned off the burner and the lights, Desiree carried the glass of milk across the kitchen and back to the elevator. She hadn't realized that she was holding her breath until the heavy brass doors slowly closed and she was on her way upstairs.

That very afternoon the local historical preservation society had proposed a plan to Desiree to help restore the Stratford to its former glory. She wondered if they would agree to a new elevator. At the rate she was going her milk would be cold again by the time she managed to return to her bedroom.

She took another sip of the lukewarm creamy liquid.

"C'mon. C'mon," she urged as if her coaxing could somehow make the vintage lift go faster.

Sometimes the darned contraption was so slow she couldn't tell whether it was moving or not.

That's when something—some gut-level feeling, some sixth sense, some basic instinct—began to niggle at Desiree. It took another twenty or thirty seconds for the fact to register entirely, however.

The elevator *wasn't* moving.

In fact, it had come to a complete stop. The numbers above the door clearly indicated that the elevator was poised halfway between the third and fourth floors.

Desiree reached out and pushed the button for the fourth floor again. Nothing happened. She tried a second time, and again nothing happened. Then she systematically pushed all the buttons, but still the elevator didn't budge.

This was obviously not her lucky day, Desiree decided. First, she had been turned down—rejection was such a harsh word—by the man she just might be falling in love with. Then she hadn't been able to get to sleep. Now her medicinal milk was rapidly cooling off and it seemed that she was stuck in an antiquated elevator.

What was the worst-case scenario? She might have to spend a few uncomfortable hours until someone—probably the early-rising Beano Jones or perhaps the ever-punctual Mr. Modi—realized what had happened and came to her rescue.

"What else could possibly go wrong?" she said, feeling rather short-tempered.

The minute the words were out of her mouth, Desiree realized she shouldn't have tempted fate by asking.

The elevator lights flickered several times in rapid succession. She slowly breathed in and then held the air precariously in her lungs for a count of ten. The lights flickered again and then, just when she thought it was safe to exhale, they went out altogether. The elevator was plunged into darkness.

"Oh, no," Desiree softly groaned.

It was pitch-black. It was so black that she couldn't see her own hand in front of her face. She groped for the emergency button, but none of the buttons she blindly punched on the panel in front of her seemed to respond.

There was no sense in panicking. She was no longer a child afraid of the dark. She was a grown woman. The elevator might seem a little stuffy, but fresh air had to be entering it from somewhere. It was hardly airtight, after all.

Desiree kept her grasp on the glass of milk, but she could tell that her hand was trembling slightly.

"'If therefore the light that is in thee be darkness, how great is that darkness.'"

She recited aloud the verse that her great-grandfather had quoted to her those many years ago.

She wasn't darkness inside; she was light. If she

doubted that for even a moment all she had to do was think of Mathis. Handsome Mathis, brave Mathis, sexy Mathis.

Desiree tried the elevator buttons again.

There was no movement.

There was no light.

There was nothing.

What an absurd, ridiculous, dumb time for the elevator to go on the fritz.

Accidents happened.

Had it been an accident? Or had someone deliberately sabotaged the mechanism?

The elevator was old and excruciatingly slow, but only last month the engineers had assured her that it was safe, that it posed no threat to the residents living at the Stratford.

She took several more deep, calming breaths and reminded herself that she was perfectly safe at the moment. She wasn't afraid. There was no reason to be afraid.

Was there?

Desiree finished off the milk, set the empty glass down at her feet and wrapped her arms around herself. Of course, she would feel better and safer if Mathis was with her. Then a dark and lonely elevator would be neither so dark nor so lonely.

To comfort herself, she said his name out loud. "Mathis."

Was Mathis safe and sound in his bed?

Was Mathis asleep?

Was Mathis dreaming of her?

Was Mathis imagining the two of them together? Was he envisioning their bodies intertwined as they kissed, touched, caressed, aroused, made love to each other?

Desiree rubbed her arms.

It was going to be a very, very long night.

Twelve

On the third attempt Mathis found the secret door. It was at the back of an ordinary broom closet on the fourth floor of the hotel, not far from the family's living quarters.

He opened the concealed entrance, peered to the right and then to the left. There was a narrow passageway running in both directions as far as the eye could see. He decided to investigate the left branch of the passageway first.

Nearly invisible in dark jeans and a black T-shirt, and wearing traditional moccasins, Mathis moved silently, stealthily, scarcely without breathing. It was a technique that he had learned and perfected during his tour of duty as an Army Ranger. In his line of work he'd found it was a skill that frequently came in handy.

It was an inside job.

George Huxley had planted the seed of the idea, of course, that first afternoon when the two of them had met in his downtown office. Desiree's godfather had been quick to inform Mathis that he suspected the incidents taking place at the Hotel Stratford were the work of someone on the inside. The former ambassador had hit the nail squarely on the head. It was an inside job, all right.

Mathis hadn't wished to alarm Desiree earlier that evening by prematurely voicing his suspicions about the hotel, but as he'd pored over the architectural drawings and the original renovation plans for the Stratford, one thing had become crystal clear to him—there were several feet of wall space unaccounted for on the fourth floor.

When had the passageway been constructed?

Who had built it?

Why had it been built?

Those were just a few of the questions Mathis would like to have the answers to. Perhaps the passageway had been conceived as a kind of priest's hole, dating back to the era of Prohibition and illegal bathtub gin, flappers and the Charleston, mobsters and their molls.

Mathis wondered where this section of the concealed passageway led. He soon had his answer. Another twenty feet and he came to a dead end at a second door.

Without making a sound he pushed the door open an inch or two. There was a small lamp, no more than a night light, really, burning on a small table in one corner. By its faint illumination he could see into a room that measured no more than six by eight feet, about the size of a walk-in closet. There was a single cot placed along one wall. It was neatly made up with a pillow and a blanket. Beside the cot was a tidy stack of magazines and newspapers. A suit of clothing hung on a nail pounded into an unfinished board.

Had someone been hiding here at one time?

Was someone hiding here now?

Yes.

Thumbtacked to the opposite wall was a calendar for the current year with each day methodically marked off with a large, red X. There was also a coffee mug and a plate on the table, along with the remnants of someone's recent dinner.

Fragments of a conversation he'd had last week with Beano reran in Mathis's mind.

''We've got a problem, boss.''

''What kind of problem?'' Mathis had asked that afternoon in the hallway between the kitchen and the hotel lobby.

''The lamb chop kind'' had been the cook's reply.

''Would you like to explain that?''

''I'm missing two leftover lamb chops from last night's dinner. The night before last half a pot of beef stew disappeared. The night before that it was a veal cutlet.''

Mathis had summed up the problem. *"Someone is systematically stealing food from the hotel larders."*

Beano had agreed. *"That's about the size of it."*

Mathis had confessed to his friend and sidekick, *"I've had my suspicions. The missing food cinches it."*

"Cinches what?"

"My theory."

"Care to tell me what your theory is?" Beano had inquired.

"This whole business has been an inside job."

Damn, Mathis swore silently, he'd been right again. Someone was literally living *inside* the Stratford. And he had a pretty good idea of who the culprit was, too.

Right now, however, it was time for him to search the other branch of the passageway.

Retracing his steps to the original broom closet, Mathis followed the narrow corridor in the opposite direction. Again, after some twenty or thirty feet by his calculations, he encountered a dead end.

He frowned and rubbed the back of his neck. Then he realized there were two small round holes drilled into the wall at eye level. Well, not his eye level. He was apparently somewhat taller than the original Peeping Tom.

Mathis crouched down the best he could, settled his face against the inner wall of the passageway and positioned his eyes in line with the holes. He blinked several times in rapid succession. It took a single heartbeat for him to recognize that he was staring into what had once been Jules Christian Stratford's study.

The view of the room was clear if incomplete. The spy holes, Mathis realized, were cleverly disguised on the other side as part of the wallpaper pattern.

So, there had been someone watching and listening as Desiree had shown him the note and the dagger. There had been someone with his or her face pressed to the wall just as his was at this very moment. And, as he had suspected, the noise he'd heard that morning had come from *inside* the wall.

Mathis straightened.

Had Colonel Stratford known about the peephole? Somehow Mathis didn't think so.

But, if the old gentleman had been aware of its existence, he'd apparently never seen fit to inform his great-granddaughter. Which didn't mean, of course, that the Colonel hadn't told anyone else.

If there was any good news about discovering a spy in their midst, it was that the secret passageways didn't extend into the bedroom wing of the family living quarters. At least those rooms were guaranteed their privacy.

Mathis had seen enough for one night. He quietly made his way back along the cramped corridor, reentered the broom closet, closed the secret door behind him and sauntered out into the hotel hallway. It was time to get a few hours of shut-eye.

He was headed for his room when he noticed that the door to Desiree's bedroom was ajar and the light was on.

Mathis hesitated. He'd already walked out on the lady once tonight when his famous self-control had started to slip. Maybe it would be better if he left well enough alone.

Damned if he did. Damned if he didn't.

Mathis raised his hand and tapped his knuckles lightly on the doorjamb. There was no response. He knocked again and softly called out her name. "Desiree, are you awake?"

Silence.

He gave the door a nudge. It slowly swung open all the way. The lamp on the bedside table was switched on. The covers were thrown back. The bed was empty. The bedroom was empty. Desiree was nowhere in sight.

Mathis glanced at the clock on the mantelpiece. It was two o'clock. Where would the woman be in the middle of the night?

He went down the hallway to the bathroom located between their two bedrooms. It was vacant, as well. Then he quickly double-checked the rest of the living quarters.

Desiree wasn't to be found.

Mathis Hazard was starting to get *that* feeling in the pit of his stomach. It wasn't a good feeling. In fact, it was a bad feeling. One that he didn't care for at all.

He made fists on his hips. "Where in the hell is she?" he demanded of the empty hotel corridor.

There was no way he could blithely go back to his room and ignore Desiree's unexplained absence. He wouldn't sleep a wink until he knew that she was safe and sound in her own bed.

Or, better yet, in his bed.

"Damn. Damn. Damn." Mathis swore under his breath all the way to the elevator.

He punched the button.

Nothing happened.

He tried again.

Again there was no response.

He glanced up at the antiquated number system above the brass doors. The arrow was midway between the three and the four.

"What the...?"

Uneasiness made Mathis shift his stance. The elevator appeared to be stopped between the third and fourth floors. Had there been some kind of malfunction? Was the vintage contraption stuck between floors?

Then an unpleasant possibility hit him. What if Desiree was trapped in the elevator?

Mathis tried to force the doors apart with his bare hands, but it was to no avail. He needed something to use as leverage. Then he remembered the broom closet. He recalled seeing an industrial mop with a metal handle that just might do the trick.

He was back in under two minutes with the mop, a heavy-duty screwdriver with an inch-thick shank and a flashlight. He used the tip of the screwdriver as a wedge, creating a small crack between the elevator doors. Then he employed the mop as a lever and forced the doors open the rest of the way.

Mathis gazed into the darkness. He switched on the flashlight and shone it down into the elevator shaft. There, some five or six feet below him, was the top of the elevator.

He cupped one hand around his mouth and called out her name. "Desiree."

He stopped and listened for a response, any kind of response. There wasn't any.

He tried again, calling out even louder. "Desiree, are you down there?"

This time Mathis thought he heard a muffled sound, but he wasn't certain. If Desiree was trapped, there was only one thing for him to do. He had to climb down and get her out.

He stuffed the flashlight and the screwdriver into the rear pockets of his blue jeans, turned his back to the gaping hole, dropped to his haunches, got a firm grip on the mop handle that he had wedged between the elevator doors and eased himself over the side. The muscles in his arms and shoulders tensed with the effort as he slowly lowered himself the five or six feet to the deck of the elevator.

His feet made contact.

He quickly assessed the situation. The beam from the flashlight revealed a two-foot-square grate in the top of the elevator. Mathis unscrewed the bolts securing the corners, slipped the tip of the screwdriver under one edge and pried up the piece of metal.

"Desiree?"

Her voice came out of the pitch-black below. "Mathis, is it really you?"

He could hear the immense relief in her voice.

"It's really me," he reassured her. Then he inquired, "Are you all right?"

"Yes." But she didn't sound all right. She sounded tired and perhaps a little frightened. She went on to state the obvious. "The bloody elevator is stuck."

"I figured as much."

Mathis shone the flashlight into the darkness below. Desiree was standing directly beneath the opening.

"I'm going to get you out," he announced.

"Good," she responded succinctly. Then she took a deep breath and asked, "When?"

"Now."

She frowned. "How?"

In a matter of seconds, he had evaluated his options. There were basically only one or two to choose from, anyway. "I'm going to reach down with both of my hands and lift you out."

Desiree made a face. "I weigh too much."

"You don't."

"I do."

Mathis dropped to one knee beside the open grate. "How much do you weigh?"

She hesitated, then answered, "One hundred and twenty-five pounds."

"In that case, I can manage," he reassured her. "I'll have to put the flashlight down, so stay exactly where you are. When I give the word I want you to raise your arms as far over your head as you can. Is that understood?''

''Understood,'' she echoed.

''On the count of three, then.'' Mathis counted aloud, ''One. Two. Three. Reach, Desiree.''

Desiree reached up. He grabbed hold of her hands and pulled with all of his considerable might. The next thing he knew she was in his arms and clinging to him for dear life.

It was a minute or two before Mathis could bring himself to point out to her, ''Much as I would like to stay exactly as we are, honey, I'm not sure how safe it is to be standing on top of this contraption.''

Desiree nodded.

''Up you go,'' he urged, giving her a hand up into the opening above them.

Once she was safely out of harm's way, Mathis pulled himself out of the elevator shaft. It was only then that he noticed his T-shirt was soaked through with perspiration. Desiree didn't seem to notice or care. She went to him, wrapped her arms tightly around his waist and pressed her face to his chest.

''Your heart is pounding,'' she finally mumbled.

It was.

''So is mine,'' she added.

She was right again.

He held her. He stroked her. He pressed his lips to her forehead. He nuzzled her neck. He buried his mouth in her hair. He murmured soft, sweet words of comfort.

It was some time before Desiree lifted her face and gazed up at him. "Thank you."

Mathis smiled down at her. "You're welcome."

"I thought I'd be stuck down there all night," she admitted with a shiver. Then she asked, "How did you realize where I was?"

Mathis condensed the rather extensive events of the night. There would always be time later to relate to Desiree what he had discovered within the walls of the Stratford.

His tone was conversational. "I noticed that your bedroom was empty, so I went looking for you. Then I spotted the elevator hovering between the third and fourth floors."

"So you put two and two together..."

"And came up with a version of four." After several moments, Mathis asked, "What happened?"

Her voice was jagged. "I couldn't sleep. I went downstairs for a glass of warm milk. On the way back the darned elevator just seemed to conk out."

He wasn't going to interrogate Desiree to find out if she thought it was purely an accident or a deliberate act of sabotage. That would just make her all the more apprehensive.

"I'll take a look at the mechanism first thing in the morning. Right now it's time you were in bed," Mathis announced.

He intended to escort Desiree to her room. And tuck her in. And see to it that she stayed there. He wasn't taking any more chances with her safety.

They reached her bedroom door.

"It was hard work pulling me from the elevator," she said.

"I was happy to oblige."

"Your T-shirt is wet," she observed unnecessarily.

He glanced down. "So it is."

Her eyes grew huge and round as saucers. "Maybe you should take it off."

Mathis tugged the T-shirt from the waistband of his blue jeans and pulled it over his head in a single motion. "Your wish is my command." He balled up the damp shirt and threw it down the corridor in the direction of his room.

Dark jade-green eyes watched his every move. "I don't want to be alone."

Mathis took in a breath. As he exhaled, air whistled out between his teeth. "What are you trying to tell me?"

Desiree only hesitated briefly before saying, "I want you to stay with me for the rest of the night."

It was only fair to issue her a warning. "If I stay, you know what will happen."

"I know," she said, sounding undaunted.

His heart beat hard. "Are you sure?"

"I'm sure."

Mathis reached behind him and closed the bedroom door.

Thirteen

Why wasn't she afraid?

She wasn't afraid because this was the right time, the right place, for the right reasons and with the right man, Desiree realized. She was thirty years old and she finally knew exactly what she wanted. She wanted to make love with Mathis Hazard.

He closed the bedroom door behind him and stood there watching her with those dark, insightful eyes of his.

"Your bathrobe is...ah..." he finally said.

Desiree looked down at the green silk robe and the green silk pajamas underneath. They were both damp. The material clung to her body, outlining her breasts, clearly showing her nipples. She swallowed. "Yes. It is."

Mathis added apologetically, "I shouldn't have held you against my wet T-shirt."

The words stuck in her throat, as any words would have under the circumstances. "It's okay."

There was something different about his voice, something darker, something evocative, when Mathis suggested, "Maybe you'd better take the robe off."

"Your wish is my command," Desiree blurted out before she could think better of it.

She untied the green silk sash around her waist, shrugged off the bathrobe and tossed it across the back of a nearby boudoir chair.

He searched her face. "Nervous?"

Desiree moved her head in the affirmative. Then she turned the tables on him. "Are you?"

He nodded. Then he went on to ask, "Are you afraid?"

She moistened her lips. "Of you?"

He nodded again.

"No," she answered truthfully.

It was another half a minute before he confessed to her, "I'm out of practice."

"So am I."

"It's been a long time for me," he volunteered.

"Me, too."

"A very long time."

It had been even longer than that for her.

Mathis attempted a faintly self-deprecating smile. "Jeez, I hope I haven't forgotten how."

"It's like riding a bicycle," she piped up. "Once you learn how you supposedly never forget."

Dark eyes grew even darker. "You've heard that, have you?"

"Yes," she said huskily.

Mathis rubbed the back of his neck in what Desiree now recognized as a habitual gesture. "Well, since we aren't exactly two old pros at this, we'll have to learn all over again."

That sounded good to her.

"Together," he added.

She passed her tongue along the edges of her teeth and laughed nervously. "I'm going to make plenty of mistakes. You'll have to be patient with me."

"I will be," he promised.

She uttered her disclaimer. "I may not know the right way from the wrong way."

"There is no right or wrong way between a man and a woman who have decided to make love to each other, Desiree. There is only their way," Mathis stated articulately.

"You're not just saying that to make me feel better, are you?" she said in a rush.

"Nope."

She believed him. Perhaps because she desperately wanted to, or perhaps because she trusted him to be honest with her, or perhaps because he had said what she knew in her heart to be true.

Mathis took a step toward her. "We'll take it nice and slow and easy."

"All right."

"Like I said earlier tonight, we're two consenting

adults, but if you change your mind all you have to do is tell me and we'll stop.''

''I won't change my mind.''

''Neither will I,'' he assured her, kicking off his moccasins as he took another step toward her.

Desiree followed his lead. Her slippers went sailing several feet across the floor.

''What's next?'' she asked.

''Jeans,'' he replied.

Without taking his eyes from hers, Mathis reached down, unbuttoned the waist of his jeans and eased the zipper down. He tugged the jeans down his legs, past his knees and around his ankles. Then he shoved them aside with his bare foot.

What remained was a man dressed in a pair of very brief briefs. What stood before her was a man with a magnificent body: broad shoulders, muscular arms, narrow waist and strong legs. It was only then that Desiree also realized he was erect.

''Good...'' she whispered more to herself than to Mathis.

''Good...?''

She moved her head. It wasn't a nod and it wasn't a shake. She finally managed to say, ''Grief.''

''Good grief?''

''You told me but I didn't believe you,'' she admitted without really clarifying her statement.

''I told you what?''

''That things are larger where you come from,'' she said, trying not to stare at him.

Mathis put his head back and whooped with laughter. "I'm glad you approve."

"I didn't say I approved."

"That's right, you didn't," he conceded.

"It's not a matter of approval or disapproval," she expounded. "I'm impressed. I'm amazed. I'm..."

"Surprised?"

"Yes, I'm surprised."

"Intrigued?"

"Okay, intrigued."

"Fascinated?" he provided without a shred of modesty.

This time Desiree put her head back and laughed with delight. It felt good to laugh. She couldn't have imagined in a million years that she would find anything amusing in the present situation. Intimacy was usually so fraught with self-consciousness and anxiety.

"You make me laugh," she told him unnecessarily.

"Believe me, that wasn't my intention," Mathis countered, although his tone of voice wasn't altogether serious.

"But it feels so good to laugh," she claimed. "It feels wonderful. Why, it's almost—"

"Orgasmic," he supplied.

Her face heated. She returned to the subject at hand. "Where do we go from here?"

He pointed. "Pajama bottoms."

The pajama bottoms were discarded, but her modesty remained temporarily intact since the pajama top covered Desiree to mid-thigh.

Mathis blew out his breath. "Not fair."

"'All's fair in love and war,'" she reminded him playfully.

A hot, masculine stare caught and held her in its grip. "It's getting down to the naked truth, in a manner of speaking."

In her opinion, it was time to put both of them out of their misery. Desiree made what she considered a reasonable suggestion. "Why don't we go on the count of three?"

He agreed and counted out loud. "One. Two. Three."

Before she lost her nerve, Desiree quickly unbuttoned the front of her pajamas and tossed the green silky top aside. When she glanced up, Mathis was straightening, his briefs gone.

"Why, you're magnificent," she exclaimed.

"And you are the most beautiful thing I have ever seen," he declared in return.

"May I touch you?" Desiree asked even as she moved toward him and reached out with both hands.

Mathis exhaled on a ragged breath and gave his permission. "Anywhere you want to, lady."

She was feeling rather daring. Arching a brow, she said saucily, "Anywhere?"

Mathis had been about to repeat the word when she brushed up against his erection. His body twitched and he grimaced. She placed her hands around him and she heard him inhale sharply.

"You did say anywhere," she reminded him needlessly.

"I, ah, did, didn't I?"

"You haven't changed your mind, have you?"

"No," he answered, and then tried to smile. But the simple act of smiling seemed beyond him at the moment.

"You are splendid, Mathis Hazard." Desiree stroked him, and then went on to extol his physical virtues. "Your skin is as soft as velvet and yet you're as hard as steel. Your muscles are smooth, still I can sense an incredible strength just beneath the surface. You're very confident about yourself, but I can feel you trembling."

"I am shaking a little," he confirmed.

"It isn't from fear."

"It isn't fear. It's because I've never been so aroused in my life. I'm trying to control a body that doesn't want to be controlled." Tension was written on his handsome features. "Why do you think I walked out on you earlier tonight?"

Desiree was painfully blunt. "Because you didn't want to make love to me."

"I did want to make love to you...desperately."

She splayed her hands across his broad, muscular chest. "Then why?"

He was equally blunt. "I was afraid of losing control."

She wrapped a soft swatch of chest hair around her smallest finger. "What's wrong with losing control?"

He gave her a slightly incredulous look. "You, of all people, have to ask that question?"

She raised her eyes to his. "Neither of us likes to feel out of control, do we?"

He agreed with her assessment of the situation. "Letting go, losing control, especially during love-making, means you have to trust the other person implicitly. I don't think either of us has much experience with that kind of trust."

"We're careful people."

"We are."

"We're particular people."

"We are that, too."

"In this day and age, with diseases of all types running rampant, with quick fixes and even quicker divorces, and with a general lack of commitment in relationships, can you blame us?" Desiree's question was rhetorical.

"Nope."

"Where does that leave us, then?"

"Right here. Tonight. In this very bedroom with the two of us standing here naked and facing each other and ourselves," Mathis stated. "Will you trust me?"

Desiree stood still. "Yes."

He raised one hand and traced the outline of her face, her neck, her shoulders, then lower to her breasts. With the tip of his fingers he encircled her nipples, first one and then the other. Her body instantly responded. She was suddenly covered with goose bumps from head to toe. She shivered.

Dark eyes studied her intently. "Cold?"

She responded huskily, "Warm."

Mathis lowered his head and took her nipple between his lips and drew her into his mouth, deeper and deeper, suckling her until she could feel the erotic tug in every nerve cell of her body.

"Warm?" he muttered as he moved to the other breast.

Desiree buried her hands in his hair, grasping fistfuls of the silky dark stuff, and threw back her own head. "Hot," she breathed out.

White-hot.

Burning up.

Flames licking at her. Scorching her flesh. Consuming her. No mind. No thoughts. No willpower. No control. No good or bad. No right or wrong.

She was.

He was.

They simply were.

His mouth moved lower. His tongue dampened her already damp flesh. His hands urged her legs apart. His magical fingers became intertwined with that most feminine and erotic thatch of hair. His fingertips sought her, found her, caressed her, delved into her.

Desiree could not speak. She could not breathe. She could no longer stand.

Mathis swept her up into his arms and carried her to the bed. He stretched out above her, hovered over her, whispered into her mouth and then sank deeply into her body.

He drove into her again and again. Slowly.

Swiftly. Gently. Forcefully. It went on and on and on. Time ceased to have any significance, any meaning, any reality. There was no beginning and, for a very long time, there was no end.

"Desiree, sweet Desiree, sweet desire, my desire," Mathis murmured against her lips, his breath mingling with hers, his flesh inseparable from her flesh, two as one.

"Mathis" was all she could say, all she could think, all she could feel.

He seemed to fill her heart, her mind, her body, her very soul. He consumed her. He devoured her. He swallowed her up whole. Somehow she was as much inside him as he was inside her.

Then the moment of climax was upon them, and Desiree felt herself gathered safely within his embrace, protected within the circle of his arms, kept within the shelter of his strength, free to let go, free to lose control, free to experience, free to simply be.

She splintered into a thousand pieces yet remained whole, became more whole than she had ever been before.

The world seemed different. The world looked different. The world *was* different. She could see so clearly, smell so keenly, hear so acutely, feel so intensely.

And she was no longer afraid....

Why was he afraid?

He shouldn't be afraid but he was, Mathis Hazard realized.

He was afraid because it was the right time, the right place, for the right reasons and with the right woman. He was afraid because he desired Desiree, wanted Desiree, desperately needed Desiree.

Contrary to Beano's assertion—how had it gone? "Women...can't live with them"—Mathis was very much afraid that now he couldn't live *without* this woman.

How in the hell had he allowed that to happen?

He had always been alone. He had always been a loner. He traveled light. He lived by his wits and a finely honed set of instincts. He trusted no one but himself.

Mathis glanced down at the lovely woman beneath him on the bed and recognized that this was his moment of truth.

What was he really afraid of?

He was afraid of loving Desiree and the loneliness that could, would, overpower him when she left.

Mathis gently withdrew from her and rolled over onto his back. He lay there on the bed and stared up at the ceiling. A thousand stars twinkled down at them from the heavens. "'The night has a thousand eyes,'" he said at last.

Desiree curled up next to him, snuggling into his side. "'And the day but one,'" she quoted, pointing to the golden sun at the center of the painted mural.

His brow wrinkled in puzzlement. "How does the rest of that poem go?"

Desiree recited it aloud for him.

"'The night has a thousand eyes,
And the day but one;
Yet the light of the bright world dies
With the dying sun.
The mind has a thousand eyes,
And the heart but one;
Yet the light of a whole life dies
When love is done.'"

She turned her head on the pillow. "Is that what you're afraid of, Mathis?"

He didn't answer her question. Instead, his mind was suddenly swirling with possibilities. "Tell me again what you found in the dictionary in reference to a Bengal light."

Desiree made the leap of logic with him. "It was a type of light once used for signaling or as a flare," she explained. "Sometimes it was apparently blue in color, and sometimes it was various colors, according to Webster's."

Mathis stuffed another pillow behind his head. "And what was your great-grandfather's favorite Bible verse?"

Desiree recited it for him. "From the Gospel of Matthew, 'Lay not up for yourselves treasures upon earth, where moth and rust doth corrupt, and where thieves break through and steal: But lay up for yourselves treasures in heaven.'"

Mathis was trying to put two and two together and come up with four, but he hadn't succeeded in doing so yet. "The Colonel always told you to look to the stars, didn't he?"

"Yes."

Desiree cast a meaningful glance at him. "What made you think of that now?"

Mathis almost said the ceiling directly above their heads but thought better of it.

"The stars in your eyes," he murmured seductively, coming up on one elbow and bending over to kiss her.

Desiree laughed softly. It was a lovely sound that came from the back of her throat.

"And the heaven I've found in your arms," Mathis added for good measure, pulling her to him as he rolled over onto his back.

Desiree was splayed across his body, slender legs on either side of his, enticing breasts pressed to his chest, sensitive skin to sensitive skin, bone and muscle to bone and muscle, male and female, the same and yet so different.

The look in a pair of alluring jade-green eyes captured his attention. The touch of her mouth on his mouth, her small, pink tongue making swift little forays between his lips distracted him. The heat of her feminine desire brushing against his manhood brought a groan of arousal from deep within him.

Desiree did drive him crazy, Mathis acknowledged to himself. And he never wanted her to stop.

The mural on the ceiling overhead. The twinkling stars. His fleeting thoughts. His suspicions. They could all wait. There would be time enough later.

Much later.

Fourteen

"Are you trying to tell me that my great-grandfather meant his message literally?" Desiree remarked to Mathis later that night as she pulled on a pair of slacks and a sweater.

Mathis retrieved his jeans from the floor of her bedroom. "That's what I'm trying to tell you, honey. When the Colonel encouraged you to look to the stars, I don't believe he was referring to your future hopes and dreams or even to the celestial bodies in the heavens."

"What was he referring to, then?"

"I think he meant the stars on the ceiling directly over your bed," Mathis explained.

She was perplexed. "Why didn't he tell me so?"

Mathis arched one brow in a knowing fashion.

"How old were you when you visited the Stratford?"

"Five. Six." Desiree went on to tell him, "I quit coming after my great-grandfather died."

"Which was at age—?"

"Ten."

"You were just a kid, Desiree. Maybe at the time the Colonel told you the best way he knew how. He made it into a game. A game that you've always remembered."

"He obviously knew from the terms of his will that one day I would inherit the hotel," Desiree mused. "Perhaps he believed that somehow I'd figure it all out once I was an adult." She paused for a moment, put her head back and gazed up at the familiar mural. "What is it about the ceiling?"

She watched as Mathis dropped to one knee and retrieved his moccasins from beneath a chair. "What were the fabled Bengal Lights that your great-grandfather mentioned were part of his reward for saving the maharajah's son?"

Desiree shrugged her shoulders. "I don't know. He never explained what they were. At least not in his diary."

"Exactly."

She still didn't understand what Mathis was driving at. "What do you think they were?"

Mathis thrust his feet into his moccasins and straightened. "I think they were significant, or at least well-known, or the Colonel wouldn't have referred to them as 'fabled.'"

She couldn't argue with his reasoning. "I'd reached the same conclusion myself."

Mathis went on. "They must have been valuable or the maharajah wouldn't have regarded them as sufficient compensation for the Colonel's heroic act."

"So it's likely that the Bengal Lights were worth a lot of money," she theorized.

"Bingo."

"That still doesn't tell us what they were." Desiree wanted to throw up her hands in frustration. "We don't even know whether or not my great-grandfather kept them all those years."

Mathis paced back and forth in front of her. In the lamplight, he cast a long shadow across the bedroom wall. "Let's evaluate what we do know. The maharajah was an absolute ruler, a prince, an immensely wealthy man of another time and place who possessed numerous palaces, room after room of fabulous treasure, and riches beyond our wildest imagination today."

She knew he was right.

Mathis went to stand at the window. He pulled back the drapes and looked out for a moment, then turned to her. "The maharajah was evidently a generous man, as well. You told me that he presented a number of expensive gifts to your great-grandparents simply because they were his honored houseguests."

"That's correct."

"So if an honored houseguest then saved the life of his eldest son and heir, the maharajah might very

—

well have bestowed upon him a reward of immense proportions.''

''A Rolls-Royce for one thing,'' she reminded him.

''And an elephant.''

''And the fabled Bengal Lights.'' Desiree gazed up at the ceiling again. A vague notion was starting to take shape in her mind. She slowly lowered her head and looked at Mathis, her lips parting, her eyes growing even larger.

She began to think out loud. ''A Bengal light was a blue light or various colored lights used for signaling. Grandpapa and I used to count the points of light or stars on the ceiling. 'Look to the stars, Desiree.' Surely you don't think...''

''I do.'' Mathis made for the bedroom door.

She called after him, ''Where are you going?''

''To get a ladder,'' he informed her. He said, over his shoulder, ''I'll be right back.''

Within several minutes he'd returned with a stepladder.

Mathis seemed to know his way around her hotel better than she did. ''Where in the world did you find that?'' Desiree inquired.

''In a broom closet just down the hallway.'' Then he seemed to remember something. ''By the way, remind me to tell you about that broom closet later.''

Desiree gave him a dubious look. ''All right.''

The ladder was quickly put into position. ''Let me give it a try first,'' Mathis said to her. ''It's a high ceiling and I'll have a better chance of reaching the mural.''

She steadied the bottom of the ladder as Mathis started climbing. ''Do you have a knife or something with a sharp point?'' she asked, looking around.

He halted. ''Hand me that screwdriver.''

Desiree immediately passed it up to him.

Mathis reached the second rung from the top and stopped. He braced his weight against the ladder and examined the ceiling, studying the stars one by one. Then he inserted the tip of the screwdriver under what appeared to be the constellation Orion, the hunter, and tried to pry a piece of it loose.

Nothing happened.

''No luck?'' she said.

''Not yet,'' he called down to her.

''Try the large blue star to your right,'' Desiree suggested.

Mathis inserted the tip of the screwdriver under what appeared to be a blot of blue paint. ''This one seemed to move a little.''

''Try again,'' she encouraged him.

He exerted more pressure and the blot fell off into his hand. He slipped the screwdriver under another star and performed the same procedure. Once he had accumulated three or four pieces of the ceiling, he placed the screwdriver into the back pocket of his jeans and descended the ladder.

Desiree's heart began to pick up speed. ''What did you find?''

Mathis opened his hand.

There, in his palm, were four large convex stones, each about the size of a half-dollar. They were deep blue in color, and partially covered with specks of paint and several layers of dust and grime.

Desiree picked one up and examined it. "What are they?" she finally asked.

Mathis rubbed one dirty stone against the pant leg of his jeans. Then he held it up to the light and slowly turned it 360 degrees. "I'm no expert on gems, but I'd venture to say that what we're looking at are very large and very valuable star sapphires."

"Star sapphires primarily come from Kashmir, or at least they used to," Desiree said.

"Kashmir is in India," he added.

They both looked up at the ceiling. In unison they declared, "The Bengal Lights."

"My God, Mathis," she exclaimed with a pounding heart, "there are hundreds of them."

He took it a step further. "Maybe even thousands."

Desiree breathed in deeply and whispered, "They must be worth a small fortune."

"Actually, my dear Mrs. Hazard," said someone with a very clipped, very accented, very British male voice from the bedroom doorway, "they're worth a bloody *large* fortune."

He was a damned fool, Mathis berated himself.

He'd forgotten the first rule of "The Art of War" as set down by General Sun Tzu: "It is better to be prepared and have a strategic plan than to simply react to a situation.''

He wasn't prepared and he didn't have a strategic plan for dealing with either Rashid Modi or the nasty-looking revolver the hotel manager was pointing straight at Desiree.

''Exactly what is the meaning of this, Mr. Modi?'' the gutsy lady demanded to know.

''After a great deal of time and trouble on my part, you have done me a great favor, Mrs. Hazard.'' A sinister expression transformed the man's face. ''I have been searching for the Bengal Lights for nearly eight months and you have found them for me.''

Delicate nostrils flared. ''You knew about the stones?''

Rashid Modi nodded his elegant head. ''Why else would I be working at a second-rate establishment when I could be at a first-class hotel, making twice the salary you can afford to pay me?''

''I had wondered about that,'' Desiree admitted.

''Then you are not nearly so gullible as Charlotte Stratford when she hired me last winter. She asked very few questions and didn't even bother to check my references.''

''Then you deliberately took a position with the Stratford in order to search for the gemstones.''

The manager's smile was feral. ''As you Americans are so fond of saying, that's it in a nutshell.''

Desiree regarded him without displaying any fear. ''How did you know about the Bengal Lights?''

Mr. Modi didn't seem averse to answering her

question. "Before I ran out of money and had to go to work to support myself, I was at Oxford for a time. I shared rooms with another student from India, a young man who was a member of a very old and privileged family. Indeed, my roommate confided to me one night during a drinking binge that he was the great-great-grandson of a maharajah."

Desiree softly gasped.

Mr. Modi smiled again. It wasn't a pleasant sight, in Mathis's opinion.

"Yes, *that* maharajah," the hotel manager continued. "Anyway, the young man enjoyed telling stories. One of the stories he related to me was about a magnificent collection of star sapphires called the Bengal Lights. It seemed that they had been in his family for generations until they were given to an English officer serving in India in 1929. My research led me to Jules Christian Stratford, formerly of His Majesty's service. Since there was never any record of the gemstones being sold or auctioned off, I made my plans to come to America and find them." Rashid Modi seemed immensely pleased with himself. "And that is exactly what I did."

"Surely the success of your plan was a long shot," Mathis pointed out.

"Long shot or not, the Bengal Lights are worth a maharajah's ransom." Mr. Modi brandished his weapon. "Now, Mr. Hazard, you will hand those few paltry stones to your wife, climb back up the ladder and get to work. If your calculations are correct, there are several hundred or more stones still embedded in the ceiling.''

Mathis refused to budge.

''I assure you, I will not hesitate to shoot a woman, even one as beautiful as your wife.''

''Do you honestly believe you can get away with this, Mr. Modi?'' Desiree challenged him.

''Yes, I do.''

''But the Bengal Lights aren't yours,'' she reminded him.

''Nor are they yours,'' he insisted.

''They rightfully belonged to my great-grandfather. They are part of the Stratford. The Stratford is now mine,'' she stated.

''I will not argue the semantics of ownership with you, madam. Possession is nine-tenths of the law and the Bengal Lights will soon be in my possession.'' He glanced up at Mathis. ''You'll need to work more quickly, Mr. Hazard. We wouldn't want anything unfortunate to happen to your lady.''

Desiree wasn't finished with the man. ''Were you the one who left the note of forewarning in my great-grandfather's study?'' she asked.

Rashid Modi frowned. ''What note of forewarning?''

''I guess that answers one question,'' Mathis said from above them. ''But raises another.''

''You will keep silent. You will keep working and you will carefully hand the stones down to your wife,'' the villain instructed. Turning to Desiree, he said, "I need a receptacle in which to transport the stones. You will loan me your handbag."

Desiree put her nose in the air and sniffed with disdain. "*Loan* you my handbag? I was greatly mistaken about you, Mr. Modi. I thought you were a gentleman, and it turns out that you're nothing more than a common thief."

"In that case you'd better drop the gun, Modi, and put your hands in the air," commanded a gruff, no-nonsense voice from behind them.

With the very sharp tip of a sword prodding him in the back, Rashid Modi wisely did as he was ordered.

Desiree opened and closed her mouth without managing to utter a sound.

Mathis was relieved that he wasn't going to have to employ the screwdriver as a crude weapon, after all. Not that he would have hesitated to use the knife-like implement if it had come down to either Rashid Modi's life or theirs.

Instead, Mathis Hazard found himself grinning from ear to ear with immense satisfaction as he greeted the newcomer. "Major Bunk, I presume."

Fifteen

"I have a confession to make," Mathis told Desiree over a cup of strong, black coffee as the two of them quietly sat on the sofa in Jules Christian Stratford's study.

It was later that same morning. The night had been the longest and the most unusual of her life, Desiree reflected, but the sun was shining now and the day promised to be a particularly fine one in Chicago, perhaps the finest of the summer.

The authorities had come and gone, taking Mr. Rashid Modi away with them.

Major Bunk was reinstated in one of the Stratford's best rooms, and was being hailed by one and all as a hero. The aging gentleman and former officer had not stopped beaming since the unpleasant incident over a "few fancy baubles," as he referred to the Bengal Lights, had been successfully concluded.

Indeed, at this very moment the Major was no doubt downstairs in the dining room enjoying another piece of carrot cake under the watchful and adoring eyes of the two Miss Mays.

Mathis cleared his throat and began again. "I have to confess that I was caught off guard last night."

Desiree reached out and patted his hand reassuringly. "It happens to the best of us."

He scowled and vehemently declared, "Not to me."

She was too exhausted to pretend a coyness she wasn't feeling. "I want you to know that I have absolutely no regrets. It was wonderful. In fact, it was the most wonderful experience of my life. I'd do it again in a minute."

Mathis blinked several times in rapid succession. "I was about to confess that I did a lousy job of protecting you."

Desiree's mind searched back over the events of the previous night. In the heat and passion of the moment, had they forgotten to use protection?

She snapped her fingers together. "There's no need to worry. It isn't that time of the month for me."

Mathis's mouth disappeared altogether. "I was speaking of my failure to protect you from Rashid Modi."

Her mouth formed a perfectly round O.

He continued. "I was admitting that I'm a lousy

security agent. I completely forgot the three keys of an effective defense. I failed to identify, understand or avert the threat.'' He shook his head dejectedly. ''I'm not the man I once was. I've lost my edge. I'm permanently retiring from the business.''

Desiree knew exactly what she must say and do. ''You can't fool me, Mathis Hazard. I spied your hand on that screwdriver last night and I saw the look in your eyes. You were ready, and certainly more than able, to do whatever had to be done to defend me.'' She squeezed his hand. ''I think it was magnanimous of you to allow Major Bunk to have all the glory.'' She added with a sigh of contentment, ''It makes for a perfect ending to the story.''

''Not quite the perfect ending,'' he muttered with a degree of sardonicism.

Desiree blithely went on. ''I don't know which disclosure has surprised me most, however—finding out that it was Cherry Pye who left me the melodramatic note of warning because she suspected there was something not quite cricket about Mr. Modi, or the fact that Miss Pye and Beano are a couple.''

Mathis showed his teeth for an instant. ''You're forgetting two factors. Miss Pye was once on the stage and something of a performing artist.''

''And—?''

''And Beano's specialty is cherry pie.''

They both laughed lightly.

''At least the Miss Mays and the Major won't have to look for a new home,'' she said, genuinely relieved. ''The Bengal Lights will help in restoring this marvelous old hotel to its former grandeur just as my great-grandfather would have wanted."

"The Colonel would be very proud of you," the man beside her said admiringly.

"Now I have a confession to make," Desiree blurted out.

Mathis's expression was drawn. "What is it?"

"I can't bring myself to tell the old dears," she said cryptically, setting her coffee cup down on the table in front of them and wringing a fine linen napkin between her hands.

Mathis apparently required clarification. "The old dears being the Miss Mays?"

Desiree nodded her head.

"What can't you bring yourself to tell them?"

She raised her eyes to his. "I can't bring myself to tell them that I've never been to New Mexico, that you aren't going to be staying here at the Stratford to oversee the renovations and, most of all, that we aren't really married."

The tension visibly eased from Mathis's expression. "Then there's only one thing for us to do," he said to her.

Desiree was breathless. "What is that?"

Mathis declared, "We'll get married."

She was suddenly unsure of the course she had chosen. "Is it a good enough reason?"

The handsome man beside her sat back and spread his arms along the sofa. "I can name a dozen good reasons why we should get married," he claimed.

Her heart came to a standstill. "Name one."

Dark, intent eyes found hers. ''You love me.''

Desiree couldn't deny it. She did love him. She licked her lips and said huskily, ''Name another reason.''

''I love you.''

It was a beginning.

Mathis Hazard was apparently on a roll. ''I used to think that I was destined to spend my life alone. I knew my past set me apart, made me different from other men, made me alone, made me a loner. I didn't even think it odd to buy a ranch in the middle of New Mexico, located between a range of isolated mountains and a secluded lake, entirely away from civilization.'' He blew out his breath. ''I lived in a world where a man learns to need no one, where a man trusts only one person—himself. Now I need you. I trust you. I can't imagine living the rest of my life without you beside me.''

Those were all good reasons, Desiree decided.

Mathis was suddenly down on one knee in front of her. ''Will you marry me, my love?''

Desiree blinked away the tears of happiness and replied, ''I will marry you.''

He stood and held out his hand to her. ''We didn't get much rest last night.''

She placed her hand in his. ''No, we didn't.''

''How about a well-deserved nap?''

Desiree looked at him. ''I don't think I could sleep in the middle of the day.''

There was a light in Mathis's eyes and it was shining brightly. ''Who said anything about sleep....''

A Word About Sapphires

At one time, the finest sapphires came from Kashmir in India. The largest star sapphire in the world is the 563-carat ''Star of India.'' After more than three centuries of indefinite history and ownership, it is on display at the American Museum of Natural History in New York City.

The star sapphire is called the ''stone of destiny'' because the three lines forming the brilliant center represent faith, hope and charity.

* * * * *

COMING NEXT MONTH

#1225 PRINCE CHARMING'S CHILD—Jennifer Greene
10th Anniversary Man of the Month/Happily Ever After
Pregnant? Impossible! Nicole Stewart knew she hadn't done *anything* that could get her pregnant! Of course, she did have some passionate memories of being in handsome architect Mitch Landers's strong arms.... But that had been a dream...right?

#1226 LOVERS' REUNION—Anne Marie Winston
Explorer Marco Esposito's knee—and career—were shot, but he was determined to discover new territories again. Then beauty Sophie Morrell walked back into his life. Sophie had always loved Marco, but could she convince him that *she* was his most exciting *re*discovery?

#1227 THAT McCLOUD WOMAN—Peggy Moreland
Texas Brides
He was determined to protect his heart. Jack Cordell had been hurt deeply once, and even though he was attracted to lovely Alayna McCloud, he would never again bare his soul to another. It was up to Alayna to show Jack that with love anything is possible....

#1228 THE SHEIK'S SECRET—Judith McWilliams
Being mistaken for his twin brother was the plan. Falling in love with his brother's ex-fiancée *wasn't!* Yet how could Sheik Hassan Rashid resist Kali Whitman's tempting sensuality? But would Kali's love endure once she learned Hassan was not the man he claimed to be?

#1229 PLAIN JANE'S TEXAN—Jan Hudson
It was love at first sight. At least for millionaire Matt Crow. But plain-Jane Eve Ellison needed some convincing. So Matt sat down in his boardroom to plan a campaign to win her heart. But Eve had other ideas...and they didn't involve a boardroom....

#1230 BLACKHAWK'S SWEET REVENGE—Barbara McCauley
Secrets!
Lucas Blackhawk wanted revenge! And by marrying Julianna Hadley, he would finally have it. But Lucas soon discovered that sweet Julianna was nothing like her cold family. Was exacting revenge worth losing this new but true love?